THE WITCHING OF THE KING

GREG HOOVER

Black Rose Writing | Texas

ISBN: 978-1-68433-707-1
PUBLISHED BY BLACK ROSE WRITING
www.blackrosewriting.com

Printed in the United States of America
Suggested Retail Price (SRP) $15.95

The Witching of the King is printed in Baskerville

*As a planet-friendly publisher, Black Rose Writing does its best to eliminate unnecessary waste to reduce paper usage and energy costs, while never compromising the reading experience. As a result, the final word count vs. page count may not meet common expectations.

I dedicate this novel to my wife Kristen and our four wonderful children, Brenden, Ethan, Sophia, and Zoe.

Acknowledgements

Many people have helped make this novel a reality. First, I want to thank my wife and children. Their patience, technical support, proofreading, and unconditional love made this novel possible. Next, I want to say a special thank you to my son Ethan. His literary feedback, excellent editorial skills, and enthusiasm have enriched my writing process. Finally, I want to thank my publisher, Black Rose Writing. Their expertise, guidance, and support have enhanced my novel.

THE WITCHING OF THE KING

"Thou shalt not suffer a witch to live."
Exodus 22:18
King James Version

CHAPTER ONE

***January 1604, on the road to Hampton Court Palace
near London, England***

Wolves closed in behind us, snarling and snapping.

"Faster!" our driver shouted as he cracked the reins, and the horses surged forward.

We sped through the moonlit forest, horse hooves pounding. Our carriage pitched back and forth as we bounced over the bumpy road. Ice crunched beneath our wheels as we raced through the fog. After a few tense moments, the bark of the wolves grew faint.

"I think we outran them, Will," said Richard Burbage. His dark hair framed his smile as it spread across his bearded face. My friend was thirty-seven years old—four years younger than me—and at the height of his acting career.

"If only we could outrun the plague so easily," I said.

The old carriage creaked as we rolled along. The scent of dried flowers filled the cab. I gazed out of the window at the barren oak trees standing watch in the moonlight. Pulling a wool blanket up over my ears, I settled back into my seat. I took a deep breath and blew on my hands, warming them.

The plague had begun the previous year and spread like wildfire across England. Some said it was a punishment from our Lord for heresy. Others said the terrible illness was the birth pangs of the Apocalypse, a harbinger of the end of days. But many feared that the Black Death had still another source—witchcraft.

"The sickness is spreading fast," said Richard, breathing out a white cloud. "If only there was something we could do about it."

"Well, our new king has made some recommendations," I said. "He wrote a book on the plague and how to fight it."

"Yes," said my wife, Anne Hathaway, her flaxen hair neatly tucked under a lace-lined shawl to keep out the cold. "And doctors try to treat victims of the plague by purging and bloodletting."

"And with vinegar, rue, and walnuts," I added. "Or with roasted onions mixed with butter and garlic."

"Stop," said Richard, smiling, "you're making me hungry. Besides, I don't know how well these measures are working."

"I'm afraid you're right," said Anne. She breathed through a handkerchief laced with vinegar, another way of protecting oneself from the contagion. "The Black Death still rages throughout the land. Fear drapes over England like the burial shroud over Queen Elizabeth."

We hit another bump in the road, rattling our coach. "And now a Scottish king sits on the English throne," added my teenaged daughter, Judith. She always had a fascination with royal intrigue.

I can still remember how Judith looked at that age. Her chestnut hair was long and shiny, even in the dim light. Her eyes were the color of dark amber tea. Judith clasped rosemary and frankincense in her hands. The new king had many such recommendations for warding off the plague.

"Well, at least King James was sensible enough to invite us to perform at the Hampton Court Conference," said Richard. His hearty laughter drew me back into the present moment. "It's wise to have something pleasant to keep the bishops and the Puritans from killing each other at that remote palace."

"Are you going to do something from your new play?" asked Judith.

"No," I replied, smiling at her. "Amidst all this gloom, it's best to perform something light—*A Midsummer Night's Dream*."

"I'm glad we are going to the palace a few days early," said Richard, looking out the window. "Since the Globe Theatre closed because of the plague, it's been difficult to earn a living. I want to have time to make sure that everything is perfect for our new patron." He turned his head and looked at me. "How is your new play coming along?"

"I think it has potential," I replied, always eager for feedback about my writing. "Have you read the excerpt I gave you?"

"Yes," said Richard, smelling the sweet scent of the herbs in his hand. "To be or not to be, that is the question: Whether 'tis nobler in the mind to suffer the slings and arrows of outrageous fortune, or to take arms against a sea of troubles, and by opposing end them."

"Very good," I nodded, happy to learn that he had already committed some lines to memory. With a new royal patron, I too felt the pressure to make a good first impression for our theater company. Especially considering that he was so unfamiliar to us all.

While I was gazing out the window into the darkness, lightning flashed. Deep in the moonlit forest, there was something strange. Five figures, dressed in hooded robes, were standing in a circle. Sitting up straight, I strained to see into the night. Lightning flashed again, but this time there was nothing except an empty clearing in the foggy forest.

Our coach hit another pothole, jarring me out of my thoughts. I noticed a new actor with our theater company watching us. He was young—maybe nineteen—and he had honey-blond hair and delicate features, making him an excellent choice to play the female roles in our plays.

"I've been meaning to introduce myself," I said to our new actor. "I'm William Shakespeare," I nodded at my friend, "and this is Richard Burbage."

"Delighted to meet you both," he smiled at us. "I'm Samuel Winston." His voice was soft, again making him the perfect actor to play female roles for our company.

"Where are you from?" asked Richard.

"Bristol," said Samuel.

"Where the plague began," said Richard, glancing at me.

"Yes," Samuel raised his vinegar-laced handkerchief to cover his mouth and nose. "Our neighbor's boy was the first to succumb to the sickness. His father was a butcher on the main road between Bristol and London. The plague seems to have spread from there."

"How many died in your area?"

"Hundreds," Samuel shrugged. "Perhaps thousands."

"I fear it will be tens of thousands before it's all over," I said, shaking my head. "If only there was a solution."

"There is," said young Winston, blowing on his hands to warm them. "Or at least, there is according to our new king."

"And what would that solution be?"

"Why, the burning of witches," he replied.

There was a long pause. Finally, Richard broke the silence.

"I heard there has been a great deal of that to the north," he said, looking concerned.

"That's right," I said. "Our new king is enthusiastic in battling witchcraft."

"The reputation of King James has preceded him," said Judith. "A decade ago, in Scotland, the king's concerns about witchcraft lead to the arrest of hundreds of people. Many of them burned at the stake or hanged."

"I'm told he is a brilliant scholar," said Anne. "But the science of demons fascinates him."

"Yes, he even wrote a book on black magic and witchcraft lore," said Judith. "It's called *Demonology*, I think."

"That's right," said Samuel, looking out the window.

We rode in silence for a few moments, the hoot of an owl and the wheels of our coach crunching the icy snow the only sound.

"I suppose," I said, breaking the silence, "that it's only natural to seek for a cause to explain the suffering of those we love."

"Some say that the witches became a problem long before this plague," said Samuel.

"What are you referring to?" asked Richard.

"Many things," said Samuel. "Animals have died, houses have burned down, harvests have gone poorly. It's said that witches even tried to kill King James by raising storms to sink the ship he was on."

"You attribute all that to witchcraft?" I asked.

Samuel raised his handkerchief to his mouth and looked at me. "You don't?"

In the distance, a wolf howled. Not knowing how to respond to Samuel, I turned my attention to my wife and daughter.

"What are you two whispering about?" I asked with a smile, but from the glance my wife gave me, it appeared I had interrupted something important.

"Oh, the same old discussion about why Judith can't act in your plays," Anne said, her cheeks pink from the cold. "As I keep telling you, Judith, it is neither a proper nor a legal activity for a lady."

"Nonsense," said Judith, waving her hand as though to brush away the remark. "I will never understand why it's illegal for women to act on stage. Men never play female characters right. No offense to you, Samuel."

"None taken," Samuel replied. "Have you ever been to Hampton Court Palace before, my lady?"

"No," said Judith. "And I'm not sure I want to go there now."

"Why is that?" asked Samuel.

"Because it's haunted," replied Judith, a playful grin spreading across her face.

"Haunted?" asked Samuel.

"Oh, yes." Judith's eyes were sparkling. "King Henry VIII's fifth wife, Catherine Howard, haunts the palace. Henry's guards arrested her there, but she broke free. She ran screaming down the hallway towards the Chapel Royal, where King Henry was praying."

"What happened then?" asked Samuel, intrigued by the story.

"She begged for mercy, but found none." Judith turned away, and gazed out the window of the coach. "They say Catherine's ghost still runs down the gallery hallway, screaming for mercy."

"Judith," said my wife Anne in a firm tone. "That's enough."

"Don't be too hard on her, my dear," I said, reaching over and holding her hand. "This has been a tough time for all of us."

"I think it will rain," said Judith. "I can smell it in the air."

After a moment, rain pattered against the roof of our coach.

"Caused by witches, no doubt," said Samuel, "trying to stop the conference." I couldn't decide if he was serious, or making a jest.

"How long until we arrive at Hampton Court?" asked Anne.

"Not long now," said Richard, extending his head to look out the window. "In fact, I think I see it up ahead now."

I looked out the window. Up ahead was a large complex of structures, with lights in many windows. Lightning flashed, and for a moment it illuminated the end of our journey—the Great Gatehouse at Hampton Court Palace. The promise of warm fires, soft beds, and light in the darkness, lifted our spirits; there was laughter and merriment all around.

As we climbed out of the coach, our muscles stiff from the journey, something ran across the path in front of us.

"Look," Judith said, laughing with delight. "A little black cat."

"A bad omen," said Samuel, as he turned his collar up against the cold.

CHAPTER TWO

I awoke the next morning to a room filled with light.

The gloom of the night before had lifted, and the faint scent of fresh-baked bread was in the air. We arrived so late the evening before that we went straight to our rooms in the Base Court. Anne, Judith, and I shared a small room with white walls and a large window. Our daughter was sitting by the window in the bright morning light. She looked out over the frozen gardens.

"It's so lovely here, even in winter," said Judith, seeing I was awake. "I feel like a princess."

"You are, my dear," I said with a smile. "Where is your mother?"

"She's gone to find breakfast," said Judith. "Shall we join her?"

Famished, I agreed without protest. We stepped out into the hallway, and the palace was bustling with life. We made our way down the hall, hoping to find the dining room. Exquisite paintings adorned the walls. While admiring a portrait of Henry VIII, I became lost in the brushstrokes.

"Now *there* was a king," came a voice from behind me. I turned around and was greeted by the warm smile of a thin man in his late thirties. He had short black hair and a well-trimmed beard.

"Well, he certainly was…" I paused, choosing my words carefully, "of impressive carriage."

"Quite," the man laughed and introduced himself. "I'm Myles Lewis, a chief servant here at Hampton Court Palace. Is everything to your liking?"

"Yes," said Judith. "It's magnificent here, and I love the artwork."

"I'm William Shakespeare, and this is my daughter, Judith."

"Very nice to meet you both," said Myles.

"Charmed, I'm sure," said Judith. "Sir, I'm afraid we're famished. Would you please direct us to the dining hall?"

"I will do better than that, my lady," said Myles. "If you would please follow me, I will lead you there myself."

Myles escorted us down the hall to the busy dining room. People having breakfast packed the Great Hall. The sound of dishes rattling and people talking filled the air, inviting us into the room. On the walls hung beautiful tapestries, made from silk and wool, and stitched together with silver and gold thread.

Just then, the sound of a child crying filled the dining room. I turned my attention away from admiring the tapestries. On the floor, a little girl with blond hair was sitting, tears streaming down her cheeks. She held her knee, which she had skinned on the floor. A tall, heavyset man dressed as a priest came to the girl's aid. His bright smile, curly brown hair, and rosy cheeks made me like him immediately.

"Who is that?" I asked Myles.

"That's Martin Page," said Myles. "He's the new head priest, serving the king in the Chapel Royal."

Father Page reached his hand behind the girl's ear and pretended to pull a shilling from thin air. The little girl laughed with delight, took the coin, and hugged the priest. He hugged her back, his warm smile lighting up the room. The little girl's mother beamed as she thanked the priest. She and her child giggled together as they walked off hand in hand, forgetting all about the skinned knee.

"What a kind man," said Judith, smiling at me.

The scent of fresh-baked bread in the Great Hall made my mouth water. I scanned the room and saw my wife. Anne waved to us from her table, where she sat with Samuel Winston, Richard Burbage, and other members of our acting company.

"I see our friends," I told Myles. "Thank you for your help."

"My pleasure, my lord," said Myles. "Now, if you'll excuse me, I have other matters to attend to." He bowed and left the busy hall.

"I would love to work here," said Judith. "Maybe meet and marry a prince one day."

"No one you marry will ever be your equal," I smiled at her as we sat at the table with the rest of our party. "Whether they are prince or pauper."

"Look up," said Burbage, pointing overhead. "I love that hammer-beam roof."

"It reminds me of a medieval castle," said Anne. "But nice and warm."

"And dripping with enchantment," said Judith.

Warm bread rolls were on the table, along with dried fruit and hot tea. We ate together and talked about our upcoming performance.

"This is where we'll perform," said Richard, looking around the Great Hall. "I can hardly wait."

I nodded and imagined *A Midsummers Night's Dream* coming to life in this performance space. This location had great potential for theater. I dreamed of one day moving our acting company here permanently.

"It's so nice not to have that awful plague breathing down our necks," said Anne. "I wish we could stay here until it passes."

"The plague is not the only thing to fear," said Samuel. "There may be other terrors we know not of, even in this mighty palace."

"Please," said Judith, munching on a piece of dried apple. "May we enjoy the moment and not dream up phantoms to fear?"

"I agree," I said. "Besides, we have work to do to prepare for our upcoming performance."

"I'm sorry," said Samuel. "Please forgive me, my lady."

Smoke from a nearby fireplace backed up into the room. Two servants investigated to find out what was causing the problem. One of them reached inside the chimney with a metal hook and dislodged an old shoe. I thought a shoe being in a chimney curious, and even a little humorous. However, the servants now seemed more concerned about the shoe than the smoke. I wondered aloud why they seemed so upset.

"You don't know, sir?" asked Samuel, looking surprised.

"I'm afraid not," I replied, intrigued by his seriousness.

"Why, it's a way to ward off witchcraft," he said. "An old shoe carries the scent of the one who wore it. When placed in a chimney, the fire intensifies the odor and it becomes a decoy."

"You mean the witch would go after the old shoe instead of the person?" Anne asked.

"That's the belief, my lady," Samuel said, finishing his tea.

A group of young women nearby were talking together with animated faces. Their expressions ranged from terror to exhilaration. Judith went to ask them what they were so excited about. In a moment, she returned, her eyes wide and shining.

"People have just seen the ghost of Catherine Howard outside the Chapel Royal," said Judith, clapping her hands.

"A ghost?" said Richard. "What happened?"

"They were preparing for the king's noonday Communion service when she appeared in the hall. Everyone dropped what they were doing and came running to see the ghost. I'm going! Who wants to go with me?"

"I do," said Samuel. "That is, if Master and Lady Shakespeare permit it."

I glanced at Anne, and she nodded her approval. Samuel was young, and I felt that since our performance was still a few days away, he had time this morning to have a little adventure. Besides, I was glad to have someone to look out for Judith in the busy palace.

"Enjoy yourselves," I said, remembering what it was like to be young.

"Come on," Judith took Samuel's hand and pulled him behind her. "I hope we're not too late!"

A stately woman came over to our table. She looked to be in her early fifties, and her red hair was greying.

"Pardon me," she said. "My name is Lady Sarah Goody."

We introduced ourselves and asked her to join us. She agreed and sat next to my wife. Anne poured Lady Goody a steaming hot cup of tea. I noticed that the hall was clearing of diners. It would soon be time to build the set for our performance.

"The reason I wanted to speak with you is to ask you about the man who left with the young lady." Lady Goody took a sip of her tea. "He looks very familiar, but I don't remember where I know him from."

"That's Samuel Winston," said Anne. "He is a new actor with the *King's Men*."

"Oh, you're with the *King's Men*!" Lady Goody seemed pleased. "I saw you perform at the Globe Theatre three years ago."

"How wonderful," said Anne. "And you think you know Samuel?"

"Perhaps," said Lady Goody, sipping her tea. "But I don't know where I know him from."

"Could it be that he merely looks like someone you know, my lady?" I asked. "A helpful feature of a successful actor is to have an appearance that can be easily mistaken for someone else."

"Yes, perhaps," said Lady Goody. "But I don't think so in this case. Oh, this will drive me mad!"

"Well, I hope you can join us for our upcoming play," Richard smiled.

"Yes, I plan to," said Lady Goody, smiling. "Now I must go. Very nice to meet you."

"Our pleasure," said Anne. "May I walk you out?"

"Thank you," said Sarah Goody as she finished her tea. She stood, smoothed her dress with her hands, and left the hall with Anne and the last of the diners. I was glad my wife was making friends here.

Richard and the other actors began setting up for the play, and a few servants helped rearrange the chairs and tables. We had brought basic scenery with us, and we all joined in building the set for *A Midsummers Night's Dream*. I've always loved the sounds of setting up for a performance. Richard felt the same way. His face had a look of almost mystical rapture.

We needed rope to secure scenery, so we asked a servant where we should look for some. He directed us to a nearby storage room; Richard and I made our way there together.

"What do you think of our new actor?" asked Richard.

"Samuel?" I asked. "He seems fine. Perhaps a bit melancholy."

"Yes," said Richard as we entered the storage room. "But with the plague beginning so close to his home, that's understandable."

"Yes," I said, lighting the stub of a candle to search the dark room. "Besides, being dramatic is part of being an actor."

Assorted boxes and supplies filled the room. Richard sneezed, startling me.

"Oh, bother!" said Richard. "It's so dusty in here!"

We began searching for the rope, but had difficulty finding it in the crowded storage room. We only had limited time, because our small candle stub was about to burn out. Richard moved two large boxes, opening access to a space with lots of assorted items. We found wooden pegs, nails, and tacks, but not rope.

We had almost given up our search when Richard at last found a coil of rope, entwined in a pile of kitchen supplies. When he pulled it free, something dropped to the floor. I reached down, picked it up, and turned it over in my hands. It was a small wax doll. The waxen figure was about four inches tall and had a crown on its head. There was a small stake stabbing it in the heart.

"Look at this," I said, moving the candle closer to the wax figure. "It has a word scratched into it."

"Let me see that," said Richard, taking the wax doll and candle. "It says, *James*."

"What do you think it is?" My skin crawled.

After a long pause, Richard lowered the wax figure and looked at me. The flickering light from the dying candle illumined his face. There was something about his expression that filled me with dread.

"It's a witch's poppet," said Richard, just as our candle died out.

CHAPTER THREE

"What should we do?" I asked Richard as we walked back towards the Great Hall.

"Do?" he asked. "Why should we *do* anything?"

"The witch's poppet is an effigy of the king," I said, looking at the wax figure in my hand.

"Is it?" said Richard. "Besides, we have a job to do. We only have a few days to build the set for *A Midsummers Night's Dream* and rehearse the show."

"We have an obligation to His Majesty," I said as we entered the Great Hall. "His life could be in danger."

"Perhaps you're right," said Richard. "You go report this to the king, and I will supervise work on the set."

I was a little disappointed. I would have preferred if we went to tell the king together. But knowing he was right, I agreed. We said goodbye, and I noticed two servants, one male and one female. I hoped they could direct me to the king.

"Pardon me," I said, walking up to them. They were both older and heavyset. "I would like to request an audience with His Majesty the King."

"What did he say?" the man asked the woman. He munched on a piece of bread he found while cleaning up a table from breakfast. His grey hair was unkempt for a servant at Hampton Court Palace.

"He asked if we found a *ring*!" shouted the woman into the other servant's ear. She smiled at me. "My husband is as deaf as can be."

"Not a ring," I replied. "I request an audience with *the king*."

"We haven't found a ring," said the man. "But if we do, we'll let you know, my lord."

"Right," said the woman. "Never keep something that's not yours, that's what I always say. Nothing we're not privy to, that is." She elbowed her husband. "Right Henry?"

"Right Alyce," said the man as he finished his bread. "The privy is right over there, my lord," he said, pointing to the side entrance.

"Not a *privy*—"

"Pardon me, sir," came a man's voice from behind me. "My name is Thomas Winter, and this is my brother Robert. May I be of assistance?"

The man speaking was in his early thirties, with curly-brown hair and a matching beard. Next to him stood a similar-looking man, but slightly older. Their family resemblance was unmistakable.

Henry, the male servant, interrupted before I could answer. He pointed at me and whispered in a loud voice, "He desperately needs a privy, sir."

"No, I don't," I replied, irritated.

"Now, now," said Alyce, the lady servant. "No need to be embarrassed, my lord. From the high king to the lowest peasant, we all share the same throne."

"Indeed," I responded, and turned to Thomas Winter. "Sir," I said, hoping the two elderly servants would go back to work. "I wish to request an audience with the king. Would you be so kind as to assist me?"

"And who exactly are you, sir?" asked Thomas.

"I'm William Shakespeare, sir."

"Never heard of you," said Robert, looking annoyed. "Come Thomas, we have business to attend to."

"You're with the *King's Men*, correct?" asked Thomas, ignoring his brother.

"I am, my lord," I said, bowing my head. "Where might I find His Majesty?"

"I'm told the new king is fond of theater," said Robert, looking at his brother.

"Yes, I'm sure we could arrange something," said Thomas. "Think of Hampton Court Palace as a giant spider's web, with the king sitting at the center. Rather than getting trapped in his bureaucratic web, I suggest you wait for him outside the Chapel Royal. He's invited a select group of

Puritans, bishops, and priests to attend a private Holy Communion service with him. It's scheduled for noon."

"I don't want to intrude," I said, not wanting to make a bad first impression with the king.

"I will send a servant to arrange a meeting with him for you," said Thomas. "I'm sure it will thrill him to meet an actor with His Majesty's new theater company."

"Thank you," I said, smoothing my hair in anticipation of a meeting with the new king.

"Our pleasure," said Robert.

Thomas Winter gave me directions. Then he and his brother went on their way, whispering to each other. I started towards the Chapel Royal. As I was leaving the Great Hall, the servant Alyce yelled to me from across the room, "The privy is the other way, sir! The other way!"

***

The hallway leading towards the Chapel Royal was quiet. The noise of the bustling palace had faded, and there was an eerie calm. It was colder in the hallway than one would have expected, and there was an unpleasant odor which I couldn't identify. I looked at an exquisite painting of Queen Elizabeth, called the *Rainbow Portrait*. I became lost in the image of Her Majesty, preserved in the prime of her life. Her regal outfit, pale skin, and flaming red hair were striking. She looked quite different from the frail queen I remembered. I noticed what seemed to be a dragon or a serpent on one of her sleeves.

"A dragon is a symbol of wisdom, they say," came a woman's voice from behind me.

I turned around, and there was a lovely young woman dressed as a nurse. She had long dark hair, piercing blue eyes, and a warm smile on her face.

"Did you know her?" I asked.

"Oh my, yes," said the nurse. "She was such a lovely young woman."

"I would imagine," I said, picturing the elderly queen the last time I saw her before she passed into eternal life.

"It's nice to see her again," said the woman, admiring the painting.

"Pardon me, madam," I said. "I seem to have forgotten my manners. I'm William Shakespeare."

"A delight to meet you," replied the woman, smiling. "I'm Sybil Penn."

A man cleared his throat behind me. I turned around to find Myles Lewis, the servant whom I had met earlier that morning, looking concerned.

"Is everything all right, sir?" he asked.

"Yes, of course," I replied. "I was speaking with the young lady."

Myles looked at me for a moment, unblinking. "And what young lady is that, sir?" he asked.

"Myles Lewis," I said. "This is Sybil Penn." I turned and gestured to where the young woman had been standing, but she was gone.

"Sir," said Myles. "Are you making sport of me?"

"She was here a moment ago," I said, confused. "She appeared to be a nurse by her dress."

"My lord," said Myles, looking serious. "Sybil Penn was a nurse to Queen Elizabeth here at Hampton Court Palace. She bravely cared for the Queen when Elizabeth had smallpox, but Sybil contracted the illness herself. She gave her life caring for Her Majesty."

"I don't understand," I said, wondering if I had missed something.

"She is a ghost, my lord," said Myles. "Guests report seeing her from time to time in the palace."

A cool breeze passed by my cheek, and I shivered. Not long ago, my daughter left for this very hallway. Reports of the ghost of Catherine Howard drew her here, like a moth to a flame. I worried about her.

"Come, sir," said Myles. "His Majesty has invited you to attend a private Holy Communion service in the Chapel Royal."

***

The sheer beauty of the royal chapel was remarkable. Overhead was a gorgeous vaulted ceiling, and the stained glass was exquisite. Incense wafted gently throughout the chapel. The king's private pew looked down on the nave. Sitting in the pew, eyes shut in private prayer, was a well-dressed man. He had curly auburn hair and a short, pointed beard, not unlike my own. I could tell at once it was the king.

The service began, and the voices of the choir filled the air, resonating throughout the chapel. I looked around me at the thirty or so fellow worshipers, and I noticed a few faces I recognized. There was Archbishop Whitgift, dressed in elegant clothes. Next to him was Richard Bancroft, the anti-puritan. There were also several well-known Puritans. They were gathered around John Reynolds, the president of Corpus Christi College at Oxford. It was certainly a diverse group.

Father Martin Page, the priest who comforted the little girl with the skinned knee, was the Celebrant. The liturgy flowed along smoothly, through the various Scripture readings, Collects, and music. I felt inspired as we moved through the worship. We were preparing spiritually, step by step, to receive Communion together as one body. This diverse group of believers coming together in common worship gave me hope for the future of England.

"Likewise, after supper he took the cup," said the Father Page, lifting the chalice.

Some Puritans looked away from this liturgical action. "Priestcraft," one of them whispered.

"If you please," someone muttered. "This is neither the time nor the place for petty politics."

"And when he had given thanks," the Celebrant continued, "he gave it to them, saying, Drink ye all of this, for this is my blood of the new testament which is shed for you and for many, for remission of sins: do this as oft as ye shall drink it in remembrance of me."

The priest lifted the chalice to his lips to receive the Sacrament. A man sitting with the Puritans spoke out in a loud voice, startling me.

"Pardon me," he said. He was a middle-aged man with short-black hair and a patchy beard. "His Majesty should have the honor of receiving the chalice first."

"No, please," the king spoke, rising from his pew. "The upcoming Conference is to determine possible changes in English worship. But for now, please continue according to the rubrics of the *Book of Common Prayer*."

"Your Majesty," said a young man. He had blond hair and a long beard and dressed as a priest. "In this case, I have to agree with the Puritans. Please do us the honor of receiving first."

"Please continue," said King James to Father Page. "We will have no more disturbances during worship."

The priest continued with the service and took a sip from the chalice. He cleaned the rim with a small square of white linen. He then turned to the assisting priest and offered him the Sacrament. Before his assistant could drink, however, Father Page began coughing. His coughing became more violent and his face turned bright red. His assistant reached out to help him, but Martin Page collapsed onto the floor. The assisting priest knelt over the fallen body and then called out, "Lord have mercy!" He made the sign of the cross, horror spreading across his face. He then looked at us and shouted, "Help him!"

We ran to the chancel steps and gathered around the priest lying on the floor. His face was now purple, his tongue badly swollen, and his eyes were squeezed tight. His hands were clenched and locked. He wasn't moving. The royal physician, an elderly but spry man, pushed his way through the small crowd. He bent down to examine the victim.

"He is dead," said the physician. "And what is more, he has been murdered."

CHAPTER FOUR

"Murder most foul," said a voice from behind me. I turned and saw it was King James.

"I'm afraid so, my lord," said William Butler, the court physician. "I've seen the purple face coloring, swollen tongue, and twisted hands before. He was poisoned."

"Hemlock, I would suppose?" asked the king, kneeling down to inspect the victim's face.

"I don't think so, Your Majesty," said the physician. "I believe he was poisoned by hebenon."

"Hebenon?" asked the king.

"Yes," said the physician. "I once examined the body of a man murdered by his wife; she poured a little hebenon in his ear as he slept."

"So, drinking it would be quite effective," I said. "And very rapid."

"Indeed," said Butler, standing up to face me. There was the odor of strong liquor on his breath; this surprised me, considering it was only noon. "Swift as quicksilver," he said, "it courses through the natural gates of the body."

"Provide him with ministrations for the time of death," said King James to the assistant priest. "After that, have him taken to the physicians' room for further examination."

"Yes, my lord," said the young priest, wiping his sweaty brow with his sleeve.

"No one here is to speak of this to anyone without my permission," said the king. "Do I make myself clear?"

We all murmured our understanding of the king's directive.

"I would like to speak to you in private," the king said to me.

"Of course, my lord," I stammered, surprised that he wanted to speak with me. My stomach tightened.

"Walk with me, please," said King James, and he turned to leave the chapel.

I lagged a moment, still unsure about his intentions.

"Now, good sir," said the king in a firm voice, and so I followed him out of the Chapel Royal.

As we walked down the hall towards the Great Watching Chamber, the king surprised me again by chatting about theater. He asked me minor questions about the art of acting. He even asked if he could call me "Will." My stomach relaxed. The king gave orders to the Yeoman of the Guard who stood watch at the door that we not be disturbed. My nervousness returned as we entered the Great Watching Chamber.

The room was spacious and beautiful, with a warm fire, plush chairs, and a thick carpet. It had a gilded ceiling, and King Henry VIII's coat of arms was still there. It would have been wonderful to inspect the various paintings on the walls, but now was not the time.

"I was told that you had something important to tell me," said the king. "Does it relate to the murder of the priest?"

"No, my lord," I said, reaching into my pocket. "I mean, I'm not sure, my lord."

"Please speak candidly, good sir," said the king.

"I found this in a supply room." I pulled out the wax figurine and showed it to the king. "Do you know what it is, my lord?"

"Indeed," replied the king, taking the wax figure from me and inspecting it with great interest. "It is a witch's poppet."

"Yes, my lord," I said.

"And it has my name and a crown on it," said the king, fascinated by the poppet. "And a knife through my heart."

"I'm afraid so, Your Majesty," I said.

"Do you think the killer meant the poisoned chalice for me?" asked the king.

"I don't know, my lord," I said. "Perhaps."

"Will," said the king. "An assassination attempt is serious business. And I'm in a difficult situation. I can't trust anyone here at Hampton

Court. If word leaks out about the murder of the cleric, it will jeopardize the success of the conference. It may even touch off a civil war."

The king wasn't exaggerating. England was like a stack of dried firewood, and all it needed was a tiny spark to burst into flames.

"I wish I could help you, my lord," I said, not knowing what else to say.

"Ah," said the king. "But you can."

The king crossed the room and poured a glass of red wine. He offered a glass to me, but I declined. He then sat by the fire, lost in thought for a moment. He raised his glass to take a sip of the wine, and then stopped, perhaps remembering the recent incident. He sat the wine glass on a nearby table and stood to face me.

"I want you to investigate this murder for me," said the king.

"Your Majesty has better trained staff for this matter than me, my lord," I said, surprised by his request.

"That's just it, Will," he said. "I can't trust any of my staff. I need an outsider. I need you."

"I'm flattered, my lord," I replied. "But with the upcoming performance and commitments to my family, I'm afraid that I don't have the time."

"Are you refusing your country in her hour of need?" asked the king. "And not only your king and country, but the royal patron of your theater company?"

I winced. With the Globe Theater closed because of the plague, we were all in terrible financial shape. How would I feed my family, and what about the other actors in the *King's Men*? We needed the support of our new royal patron more than ever. Also, I was hoping to keep Anne and Judith safe here at the palace. Here they were far away from the plague. For all these reasons, I needed the support of King James.

"My lord," I said, "it would be an honor to help. However, I don't have the authority to investigate."

The king sat at his desk, took out a parchment, quill, and ink, and began writing. He was silent for a few moments as he worked. He then stamped the letter with his royal seal and held it out to me. I took the letter and read it. It gave me the king's authority to investigate matters on his behalf. I noticed he also gave me a title in the letter, *Witchfinder General*. I winced again.

The king handed me an envelope, and he smiled with satisfaction. I folded the fine paper, put it in the envelope, and placed it in my breast pocket.

"Now you have the authority, Will," he said, and shook my hand. "Start your investigation by interviewing William Butler. He was the physician who was at the murder."

"I shall, Your Majesty," I said, trying to sound more confident than I felt.

"I suppose I should warn you he is unusual, unconventional, and seldom sober," said the king. "But he is without a doubt the finest physician in England."

The king walked over to the fire and warmed his hands. I joined him, realizing how cold my hands were, which is how they often felt when I was nervous.

"He came to my attention last year," said the king. "He revived a clergyman from a coma by placing him inside a freshly butchered body of a cow. Now *that* is medicine!"

"I would imagine that woke him up, my lord," I said.

"Yes," the king smiled. "And I realized then that I wanted this physician at Hampton Court this winter."

"Thank you for your guidance, Your Majesty," I replied, nodding, and started to leave.

"One more thing, Will," said the king. "This conference is very important. The conflict between the Anglicans and the Puritans is at a boiling point. The results of this meeting could impact Christianity for a thousand years. Your investigation needs to be quiet, quick, and independent; I have my hands full with the conference." He looked at me with a firm expression. "Do I make myself clear?"

"I understand," I bowed my head, excused myself, and stepped out of the Great Watching Chamber. I had a lot of work ahead of me and could expect no help from the king or his staff.

Lord, I prayed as I walked down the hallway, heading towards the physician's chambers. *The last thing I wanted was an adventure.*

***

I knocked on the door to William Butler's examination room. There was a loud crash, and a man's voice said, "Just a moment!" After a few more bangs, clanks, and the sound of pottery breaking, the door opened. There stood Doctor Butler, the physician I had met earlier.

"Pardon me, sir," said the doctor, brushing his white, untamed hair back with his hands. He appeared to be about seventy-years old. "I'm afraid my sight is not what it used to be, so walking through a cluttered room can be dangerous."

"Perhaps you should remove the clutter," I suggested.

"Perhaps you should mind your own business," he responded, and started to shut the door.

"Sir," I countered. "May I have a word?"

"I'm busy," said the doctor. "And I fear more of your conversation would infect my brain."

I smiled and filed the insult away for later use. The aroma from his room was strong, and I didn't relish gaining access to it.

"I'm here on the king's business," I said, handing him the letter.

Unfortunately, his hands were filthy. The clean letter became soiled as he held it a few inches from his eyes.

"May I come in, sir?" I asked, after he had a few moments to read the king's letter.

"It's not the best time," said the physician. "I'm working on the matter from earlier." He fixed me with an uncomfortable stare. "If you take my meaning."

"That's why I'm here, sir," I responded. "That's the king's business I spoke about."

The physician sighed and read the letter again, turning it over with his filthy hands.

"Perhaps it's for the best," he said finally, handing the letter back to me. "Please, come in."

I stepped into the strong-smelling room. The scent reminded me of dried herbs, but with a sickly sweet odor. Discarded candle stubs littered the table and floor. Medical books, stacked high, climbed the walls. Dozens of dusty jars filled with specimens, many of which I couldn't identify, crowded the shelves.

"What does the king think of your housekeeping?" I asked, looking at a dusty specimen jar with a preserved eel floating in it.

"He hasn't dropped by," said William Butler. "Besides, I specialize in medical research. I've been meaning to clean."

"I'm sure you have," I said, not wanting to touch anything.

"Can I offer you a cup of tea?" he asked.

"It's tempting, but no," I said, covering my nose with my handkerchief. "So, where is the victim's body?"

"Ah, you've hit upon my little problem, sir," said the doctor.

"And exactly what problem is that?" I asked.

"Well," said Butler. "I stepped away, only for a moment, to get a bite to eat, and…"

"And what, sir?" I was growing impatient.

Doctor Butler smoothed his clothes with his hands and ran his fingers through his white hair. He walked to his examination table and seemed lost in thought for a moment. Then he turned and looked me straight in the eyes.

"Someone stole the body."

CHAPTER FIVE

"You've lost the body?" I couldn't believe it. "How could anyone lose a body?"

My first instinct was to rush and tell the king, or at least his staff, about the missing body. I started to bolt from the room, but I remembered the king saying he couldn't trust his staff at Hampton Court Palace. And so, I questioned the physician and conducted a thorough search of the room, but I could find no clues. It appeared my investigation was over before it had even begun. I decided to leave the physician and question other eyewitnesses to the murder. While opening the door to leave, however, a young woman surprised me, her hand raised to knock on the door.

"Oh!" she said, startled by the sudden opening of the door. "Pardon me, my lord," she curtsied. She looked to be in her early twenties and wore a plain white cotton dress covered by a grey woolen cloak. The hood of her cloak hung down her back unused, revealing her long honey-blond hair tied with a strap of tan leather.

"Please forgive me," I said. "I was on my way out."

"I'm just bringing a few herbs that the doctor ordered," she said. "Please don't leave on my account."

"I'm not," I said, wanting to get on with my investigation. "But thank you. Please take your time."

"William Shakespeare," said Doctor Butler. "Please allow me to introduce Violet Lewis, a local herbalist."

"Nice to meet you," I said. "I'm sorry, I must be going."

"William is an actor with the *King's Men*," said the physician.

"Oh, I love theater," said the young woman, her green eyes shining with excitement. "Your acting company is building a set in the Great Hall."

"Your name is Lewis?" I asked. "Are you Myles Lewis' daughter?"

"Yes, my lord," she smiled. "My father was kind enough to help me gain employment at the palace. He found work here for my sisters, Elspet and Janet, too. Family is very important to us."

"Jolly good," I said, not wanting to waste time with pleasantries. "I must go, goodbye."

As I left the room, my conscience nagged me for being so rude. Time was of the essence, however; I could make apologies for my curtness later. I decided to go back to the Chapel Royal and look for clues. Walking towards the chapel, I thought about all the events leading up to the murder. One question haunted me. *Who were the two men who insisted that the king drink first?*

I showed my letter to the guard at the chapel door. He scanned the letter and then waved for me to enter. I stepped into the opulent chapel, and memories of the murder flooded over me.

"May I help you?" came the voice of the young priest who was preparing the chapel for the Evening Prayer service.

"Sir," I said, remembering him as the assisting priest from earlier. "I'm William Shakespeare. I'm here on the king's business."

He met me at the chancel steps, and I showed him my letter.

"I'm glad someone is looking into this ghastly business." The priest took off his Tudor bonnet and ran his fingers through his thin brown hair. "Who do you believe was the murderer?"

"I hoped that you could help me answer that question," I replied. "I'm sorry, but what is your name?"

"I'm Father Jeremiah Talbot."

"I wish we could have met under more pleasant circumstances," I shook his hand. "Did Father Page have any enemies?"

"Only every Puritan in this palace."

"I understand your point," I said. "But did he have any personal enemies that may want him killed?"

"Not that I know of," Father Talbot answered.

"Did he have any bad habits that may have drawn him into trouble?" I asked, hoping I didn't offend the young priest. "Gambling, for instance?"

"No, nothing like that," said Talbot. "At least, not to the best of my knowledge."

"May I look around the scene of the crime?"

"Of course," he said, and he opened the chancel gate.

I explored the area surrounding the altar, but it was spotless.

"Have you swept this area recently?" I asked.

Father Talbot called over an elderly man who had apparently been working in the sacristy. He introduced him as Alban Braunstone, the sexton. After introductions, Talbot asked Alban if he had swept the chancel area since the murder.

"Yes," said the old man, his long white hair flowing down to his shoulders. "I sweep the area after every service."

"Did you notice anything unusual?"

"Not especially." Alban scratched his beard. "While we were setting up for the service, there was a ghost sighting in the hall. That's not unusual, but we went to investigate, anyway."

Father Talbot shook his head. "And after one ghost sighting, others always happen in rapid succession. It's a wonder we ever get any work done."

"The palace is that haunted?"

Talbot shrugged. "People see what they expect to see."

"What about after the service?" I asked Alban. "Was there anything out of the ordinary?"

"Yes," said the man, stroking his long beard. "He had coughed up a little blood before he died. Other than that, it seemed typical."

"I'm sorry, but I have business to attend to," said Father Talbot. "If I can be of further help, please come by later. I will be happy to assist your investigation in any way I can. Until then, Alban will be happy to answer any questions you may have."

The young priest left, and I asked the sexton if he would show me the sacristy. He led me to the small room used to store items needed for the service. There were brass candle holders, liturgical books, vestments, chalices, and patens. Everything I would have expected to find in a sacristy.

"Why are there two sinks?" I asked Alban.

"One is for general use," he answered. "The other is a piscina, a sink that goes directly into the earth."

"I don't understand," I said, puzzled.

"It's for cleaning chalices so that the Sacrament returns directly to the earth," said Alban. "Rather than into the common sewer, that is."

"And that's where you cleaned the chalice after today's service?" I asked.

"Yes," said Alban. "Is something wrong?"

"Pouring the wine down the piscina was unfortunate," I said. "We lost an important clue."

"I'm sorry, sir," Alban replied. "I should have thought of that."

I nodded my head. "Can you think of anything else that may be helpful?"

"Not really," said the old man. "I wonder why someone would want to murder one of God's children."

"Some would say original sin," I shrugged. "We inherit Adam's iniquity, I suppose."

"Nonsense," said Alban. "God has given us freewill. The only thing that we can inherit from Adam is his bad example; it's up to us if we follow it."

"Then what do we gain from our Lord's sacrifice?" I asked, surprised at his candor.

"We gain his good example," said the old man. "He inspires us to make better choices. God has given us the strength to follow his teachings if we choose to do so."

"Sir," I whispered. "I would not speak so openly if I were you."

"Oh, rubbish," said Alban. "I'm eighty-seven years old. I've survived many waves of persecution. What do I have to fear now?"

Alban crossed the room and sat in a chair against the north wall. I followed him and sat in a chair opposite him. He picked up a brass candle holder and began polishing it with a clean white towel.

"How long have you worked here?" I asked.

"Twelve years," he said, concentrating on his work. "I came during the reign of Queen Elizabeth."

I picked up a candle holder and towel and began helping him polish the brass.

"When I was a young man, I was a monk," said Alban as he worked. "It was a wonderful life. I studied Hebrew and Greek, and read ancient writings, some of which are now lost. When King Henry dissolved the monasteries, however, I had to find a way of making a living. I only knew the religious life. So, I spent the last sixty years working for churches in various capacities."

He held up the brass he had been polishing and inspected it as it gleamed in the light. He seemed satisfied, set it aside, and took up another and began polishing it.

"I've served in Catholic, Reformed, and Church of England parishes," he smiled. "Depending on who was in power at the time. I have polished brass, tended cemeteries, archived manuscripts, and sewn vestments. And all the while, I listened and I thought."

"And what have you learned?" I asked, intrigued by his story.

"God more often intervenes from within than from without," he said. "God works within our hearts and within our heads. He inspires us to cooperate with him to change the world for the better. He calls us to use our physical hands to do the work that a spirit doesn't have the hands to do."

"How you escaped arrest all those years is beyond me," I said, setting down the brass I had been polishing. It was time for me to leave and to continue my search for answers elsewhere. I reached out, shook Alban's hand, and smiled. "Please do us both a favor and be careful with whom you share your religious views."

"William," he smiled back, shaking my hand. "When investigating this murder, be sure to listen to your heart as much as your head. Follow your intuitions. Trust your feelings."

"I will," I said, and turned to leave.

As I paused at the door to say a final goodbye, I noticed something lying on the floor. It was barely visible from under the edge of the piscina. I picked it up; it was a small glass vile. I showed it to Alban.

"What's this?" I asked.

"I have no idea, sir," said Alban. "I've never seen it before."

I sniffed the bottle, and the stench seemed familiar. I thought for a moment, sure that I had smelled its scent before. I sniffed the bottle again, and then I remembered.

"The smell from the hallway," I said aloud, and I sniffed the odor one more time. "And from the physicians' room."

CHAPTER SIX

What was the connection? As I left the chapel, I pondered the meaning of the vial. I was hoping the smell in the hallway would still be in the air, but it was gone. There must be a connection to it, the odor in the physician's room, and whatever was in the vial. I was hungry and thought something to eat would help me sort this out. I went to the kitchen to find out if there was any food available.

Delightful sights and scents greeted me as I entered the busy kitchen. The warmth from the ovens and cooking fires cheered me, lifting my spirits. Delicious-looking turkeys and hams were roasting over crackling fires, and dozens of servants prepared sweet delicacies. Six large ovens blazed in the kitchen, and near them were two young women, one blond and one brunette. They were covered in flour and kneading huge piles of dough.

"Pardon me," I said. "My name is William Shakespeare—"

"Oh!" exclaimed the blond who appeared to be in her late teens. "You're an actor with the *King's Men*! Our sister Violet told us she met you earlier."

"That she did," said the brunette, wiping her forehead and leaving a streak of flour. "She said that you were handsome." She then whispered something to the blond, and the two girls looked at each other and giggled.

"Violet?" I said. "Oh yes, Violet Lewis, the herbalist. She mentioned she had two sisters working at the palace."

"She told you about us?" said the blond, her blue eyes bright and cheerful. "I don't believe you!" She looked up and smiled. "What did she say?"

31

"Only good things, I'm sure," said the brunette, glancing at her sister. "My name is Janet."

"And I'm Elspet," said her sister. She extended the back of her hand towards me, almost as if she wanted me to kiss it; her sister slapped it away.

"Fancies herself a proper lady, this one," said Janet, nodding towards Elspet. "Thinks she'll be the Queen of England one day!"

Janet laughed, and her sister shot her a stern look. The two seemed to speak volumes to each other with nothing more than a glance.

Thoughts of my own daughters, Judith and her older sister Susanna, filled my mind. I wished Susanna would have joined us here at the palace, but she was an adult now and chose to stay in London. I hoped she was safe from the plague; I wished she was here to keep Judith company. And I realized that I didn't know Samuel Winston very well.

"Perhaps she will be queen one day," I said, and smiled.

"Oh, don't encourage her, my lord," said Janet, her green eyes radiant. "She's hard enough to live with as she is. Now *me*—"

"You, a queen?" Elspet laughed. "Oh, that's rich, that is. Who ever heard of a Queen named Janet? Besides, no king will marry the likes of you."

"Stranger things have happened," I said. "Pardon me, but may I have something to eat?"

"Here you go," said Janet. She handed me a fistful of raw rye dough and popped a pinch of it into her mouth as well.

"Janet!" said her sister. "He's right proper, he is. You don't serve a gentleman raw dough." She wiped her hands on her clothes. Elspet then reached behind her to a stack of fresh-baked bread cooling on a wooden rack. "Here you go, sir."

She handed me a fragrant piece of dark-brown bread. The rich scent filled my nostrils, and my hunger increased. I was about to excuse myself when I sensed someone behind me.

"Break time, ladies." It was Myles Lewis. "That is," he smiled, "if you haven't spent your entire shift talking again."

"Sorry father," said Janet, brushing the flour from her clothes. "We were helping the gentleman."

"Sir," he said to me. "May I help you find something?"

"Thank you, Myles," I said. "But your kind daughters have been—" I heard shouting in the Great Hall.

"Oh no," said Myles. "They're fighting again."

"Who?" I asked.

"The Anglicans and the Puritans."

***

As I hurried into the Great Hall, voices echoed throughout the room. Two groups of men were facing each other. One group included several priests, bishops, and their supporters. The other group had an equal number of Puritans and their followers. I noticed several faces who were present at the murder. Both men who asked the king to be the first to drink from the chalice were there.

"Please," said a regal-looking man. He was average height, with short black hair and beard. I recognized him immediately as John Whitgift, the Archbishop of Canterbury. "That's not at all what we're saying."

"That's right," said Lancelot Andrewes, the Bishop of Chichester.

"But do you believe in the doctrine of Transubstantiation?" demanded a Puritan. It was the Puritan from earlier who suggested that the king drink from the chalice first. "That the bread and wine literally become the Body and Blood of Christ?"

"Malachi," said Andrews. "There *is* a real change in the elements—"

"Sir, that's not biblical," said the Puritan, who I now knew was named Malachi.

"It is, sir," said Archbishop Whitgift. "At the Last Supper, our Lord said, 'This is my body, this is my blood.'"

"And that's not all," said the priest who had also invited the king to drink the chalice first. "Our Lord added, 'Do this in remembrance of me.'"

"You're taking the text too literally, Oliver," said John Reynolds to the young priest. Reynolds was a well-respected academic and Puritan. "And it brings up another point. We need a better English translation of the Holy Scriptures."

"We agree on that point," said Lancelot Andrewes. "Correct, Oliver?"

"Yes," said Oliver, nodding. "We need a better translation."

Now I had the names of the two men I wanted to question next.

"Archbishop Whitgift," said Malachi. "Christ also said he was 'the gate.' Was he truly a gate? He said he was 'the vine.' Was he really a vine? He was not literally a shepherd, sir. That was a metaphor."

"Metaphor depends on context," said Bishop Andrewes.

"And Scripture must be interpreted in light of both reason and history," said Oliver. "The early Church Fathers believed in Real Presence."

"Nonsense," said Malachi. "*Sola Scriptura*. Scripture alone. That's all that matters."

"That's right," said a Puritan that I didn't know. "No compromise on this point is possible."

"Then I'm afraid we're at an impasse," said the archbishop. "Gentlemen, I suggest we table this discussion until after our meetings with King James."

"I agree," said John Reynolds.

Malachi shouted at Reynolds, "We will never purify the church as long as you're so afraid of conflict!"

He turned to run out of the room and smashed into me, crushing the bread I was holding. Malachi glanced at me, and then left the room without apologizing.

"Are you okay?" asked Oliver, as the room cleared.

"Yes, thank you." I looked at the broken bread at my feet. "Oh well."

"I'm glad you're not hurt," said Oliver. He extended his hand to me. "I'm Oliver Fletcher."

I thanked him and introduced myself. After we exchanged a few pleasantries, I showed him my letter of appointment from the king. He read the letter, nodded, and handed it back.

"May I ask you a question?" I asked.

"Of course," said Oliver.

"Why did you suggest that the king drink from the chalice first?"

"For a simple reason," said the priest. "I didn't want Malachi and other more radical Puritans to gain the favor of the king before the conference even began."

"But someone poisoned the chalice."

"Yes," said Oliver. "We know that *now*."

"Do you know anyone who would want to murder Father Page?"

"Martin Page was almost a saint," said Oliver, shaking his head. "He was my mentor in seminary. When the plague first hit, he left his safe teaching position and went to serve victims of the plague. It's a miracle he didn't contract the disease."

"Only to fall victim to a vicious murderer," I said. "It doesn't seem fair. Someone told me once that God is in complete control, and either causes or allows everything that happens. Why did God cause or allow Martin Page's murder?"

"God doesn't cause suffering, Will," said the young priest. "But God *is* working in the hearts and hands of all those who are trying to ease suffering."

Alban's words from earlier came to mind.

"Consider yourself," he said. "You can solve this crime and bring a killer to justice. This will have a far-reaching effect on England. You may even stop more murders and prevent the king's assassination. But you can't do it alone. To solve this mystery, you need God." Oliver paused for a moment, and looked me straight in the eyes. "And God needs you."

I was quiet for a moment. Little did he know that I didn't relish my assignment. He had given me something to think about.

"Do you have any other questions?" asked Oliver, pulling me from my thoughts.

"Yes," I said. "Who do you believe is the murderer?"

"I don't know," he said, shrugging his shoulders. "But if I were you, I would investigate Malachi Hunter. He was the Puritan who first suggested that the king drink first. Now if you will excuse me, I have a meeting to attend."

We said goodbye, and I wanted to return to the kitchen to get another piece of bread. I was ravenous. As I turned to leave the Great Hall, people hurried through the room. Some of them seemed excited, and others afraid. It relieved me to see my daughter Judith and Samuel Winston among them.

"Judith," I called. "Over here."

"Hello, sir," said Samuel, smiling.

"This is so exciting!" said Judith, glancing at Samuel.

"What is?" I asked, as more people funneled through the Great Hall and out again. "Where's everyone going?"

"We missed seeing the ghost this morning," said my daughter. "But people are saying she could return at any moment."

Sybil Penn, the young woman I had seen earlier, came to mind. The hairs on the back of my neck stood up straight. *Could she have really been a ghost?*

"Come on," Judith said as she pulled me towards Gallery Hall. "Let's go!"

CHAPTER SEVEN

Adventurers filled Gallery Hall hoping to see a ghost. Not having any other leads, I joined them. It was cold, much colder than the connecting halls, and there was an odd scent haunting the air. It surprised me to see Richard Burbage among the sightseers.

"I was thinking," said Richard. "You should play the ghost of Hamlet's father in your new play."

"And who will you play?" I asked.

"Why, the lead role, of course," said Richard.

Smiling back, I realized that Richard was one of the few people I could trust at Hampton Court Palace. And since he already knew about the witch's poppet, I decided to take him into my confidence about the murder. I spent the next several minutes quietly telling Richard all that had happened since we last spoke. He seemed intrigued, and it pleased me when he asked if there was any way he could help.

"Oh yes, my good friend," I said. I shook Richard's hand and beamed with delight. "First, I'll need you to cover my duties related to our upcoming performances. If you have time after that, I would appreciate anything you could do on your own to help solve this mystery."

"Jolly good!" said Burbage, who always loved an adventure.

"And as fortune would have it," I said. "Malachi Hunter has just entered the hallway."

Malachi walked down the crowded hall and stopped near Judith and Samuel. He shook his head in disgust.

"Go back to your duties," he said to the crowd. "Hard work is good for the soul. The ghost showed herself this morning, but now you're just using her as an excuse to be lazy. Idle hands are the Devil's tools."

Malachi clapped his hands hard, and a few servants began leaving the hall. Richard and I glanced at each other and then went to him and introduced ourselves.

"I have no time for pleasantries," said Malachi. "Especially with loyal Anglicans."

"Sir," said Richard. "We only need a few moments of your time."

"You were in the Great Hall a few minutes ago," Malachi said to me. "You were the one with the bread."

"Yes," I replied as my stomach growled. "No need to apologize."

"Apologize?" said Malachi. "For speaking the truth?"

"I meant for running into me," I said. His mishap apparently impacted me more than it did him.

"We must purify the Church of the last shreds of popery," Malachi fumed. "I think our new king will be on our side."

"That's not why we want to speak to you," said Richard. "We are investigating the murder and assassination attempt that happened today."

"On whose authority?" Malachi demanded.

"We're on the king's business," I replied. "We would appreciate your cooperation."

"Or what?" he said. "Will the king burn me at the stake like the three-hundred protestants under Queen Mary?" Malachi paused and then added, "*Bloody Mary*."

"Queen Mary killed many faithful Anglicans," said my daughter Judith. "She even burned Thomas Cranmer, the Archbishop of Canterbury, at the stake."

"I wish she would have burned his *Book of Common Prayer* with him," said Malachi.

Judith was never one to back down from a fight. "My point," she replied with all the calm that she could muster, "is that—"

"I have no need for the opinion of a woman," Malachi yelled.

The hall fell silent, and everyone turned to watch us. I noticed that Oliver Fletcher, the Anglican priest I spoke with earlier, entered the hallway. He glanced at me and then focused his gaze on Malachi.

"Sir, I take my leave of you," said Judith and turned away.

At that moment, several things happened at once. Malachi reached out and grabbed Judith's arm, jerking her back towards him. I stepped forwards, inserting myself between him and my daughter. Samuel pressed his hands against Malachi's chest and pushed him back. Malachi recoiled for only a moment, pivoted, and punched Samuel in the face.

"Leave the hallway at once," I demanded, "or I will have you arrested."

Malachi stormed out of the hallway as Judith kneeled by Samuel. To my surprise, he was crying.

"Sir, are you okay?" came the voice of Oliver.

"Yes," said Samuel, wiping his tears from his eyes. "It's only that I have to play Juliet tonight, and now my face is all messed up."

"You look fine," said Judith. "No one will notice."

"Come," said Oliver, helping Samuel to stand. "I'll take you to the herbalist."

The three of them left the hallway together, and the crowd dispersed.

"Play Juliet tonight?" I asked Richard.

"Oh," said Richard. "Did I forget to tell you?"

"Tell me what?"

"We have been asked to perform something tonight at dinner," he replied, his bearded face showing his famous smile. "Samuel and I will perform the balcony scene from *Romeo and Juliet*."

***

Hundreds of people packed the Great Hall. I looked up at the stained glass, and the images of the Tudors in all their glory. They gazed out, forced to watch the Stuarts take their place at the royal table. Delicious scents filled the air, and the voices of cheerful people echoed throughout the room. Most of them were unaware that a murderer lurked among them.

There would be several performances that evening by various acting troupes. *The Lord Admiral's Men*, *Worcester's Men*, and several smaller theater groups, would perform. Musicians, jugglers, and other brightly dressed entertainers stood along the sides of the room. My wife waved to me, and I joined her and Richard.

Dinner was served, and a talented minstrel played the lute and sang. His songs were joyful, and for a few moments I almost forgot about the adventure in which I was snared. The food was delicious; roasted lamb, venison, and peacock, along with bread, butter, cheese, and pottage. We laughed and talked as we ate, and the plague seemed far away.

Richard took a long drink and set his cup on the table. "I was thinking," he said. "Maybe the priest wasn't murdered."

"What do you mean?" I asked.

"You said he worked with plague victims; maybe he contracted it."

"Doubtful," I said. "The timing would be too much of a coincidence. No, he was murdered."

"Who was murdered?" asked Anne, her eyebrow raised.

"Oh," I said, remembering that King James ordered me to keep this matter quiet. "Nothing, my dear."

"A murder doesn't sound like nothing," she replied.

"You may as well tell her," said Richard. "She will find out anyway."

I gave Anne a quick overview, and a concerned look came over her face.

"Where is Judith?" she asked.

"She's all right," I said, and told her about the happenings in Gallery Hall.

"My concern is for Samuel," said Richard. "That punch to his face was bad. I hope he is back stage getting ready." He glanced up at the clock in the Great Hall. "Speaking of which, I need to get into costume."

Richard left the Great Hall as *The Lord Admiral's Men* performed a scene from one of their plays. They were very good, and I became lost in their comedy for several minutes. After a hilarious conclusion to the scene, the guests applauded. I looked around the room; there were many familiar faces. Almost everyone seemed to be at dinner, each sitting with their respective group. Anglican clergy, Puritans, servants, courtiers, and the royal family, were all talking and eating together.

King James sat with his wife, Ann of Denmark. She was Queen consort of Scotland, England, and Ireland. They had three children with them who were also eating. This surprised me. It was unusual for royal children to dine at the same table as the king and queen. I looked at their lovely children and wondered about their royal destinies. Little Charles, only four years old, was playing with a napkin. It was easy to imagine a crown on his head.

Next to perform was a team of talented jugglers. Dressed in bright reds, greens, and gold, they awed the audience with their skill and discipline. After them, graceful dancers entertained us with their art. The dancers were followed by performing animals. Anne and I smiled at each other as they thrilled the crowd with their tricks.

Finally, it was time for Richard and Samuel to perform the scene from *Romeo and Juliet*. The location didn't look much like Capulet's Orchard, but a powerful performance is more important than a fancy set.

Richard Burbage entered the scene to play Romeo, and the audience erupted in applause. He was a very popular performer, and the crowd showed their appreciation. A twinge of jealousy raced through me, but I shook it off.

Samuel appeared on a makeshift balcony, dressed as Juliet.

"Poor fellow," I murmured.

"Samuel?" whispered my wife. "Why, because they didn't clap for him?"

"Not that," I shook my head. "Notice the silk scarf covering his lower face. It must be swollen from the fight."

"I'm so glad Judith wasn't hurt in that scuffle," replied Anne.

Richard knew his lines well. He seemed to pull dramatic tension and emotion out of thin air. At the perfect moment, he spoke:

"But, soft! what light through yonder window breaks?
It is the east, and Juliet is the sun.
Arise, fair sun, and kill the envious moon,
Who is already sick and pale with grief,
That thou her maid art far more fair than she:
Be not her maid, since she is envious;
Her vestal livery is but sick and green
And none but fools do wear it; cast it off.
It is my lady, O, it is my love!"

"I love this scene," whispered Anne in my ear. "I've watched it a hundred times, but I always notice something new."

"Thank you," I smiled. Anne was always my greatest fan.

"Ay me!" said Samuel as Juliet. His first professional lines on stage.

"She speaks," Richard continued, lost in character. He paused a long time. When the audience couldn't bear the tension one moment longer, his strong clear voice rang out over the Great Hall.

> *"O, speak again, bright angel! for thou art*
> *As glorious to this night, being o'er my head*
> *As is a winged messenger of heaven*
> *Unto the white-upturned wondering eyes*
> *Of mortals that fall back to gaze on him*
> *When he bestrides the lazy-pacing clouds*
> *And sails upon the bosom of the air."*

Samuel turned and faced Romeo, and spoke in a clear and realistic feminine voice:

> *"O Romeo, Romeo! wherefore art thou Romeo?*
> *Deny thy father and refuse thy name;*
> *Or, if thou wilt not, be but sworn my love,*
> *And I'll no longer be a Capulet."*

"He is quite good," said Anne. "A born actor."

"Yes," I said, impressed. "You would think Samuel had been around acting his entire life."

The rest of the scene played out perfectly. It was one of the best performances that I had ever seen of it. At the closing of the scene, the two actors took each other's hand and bowed to great applause. While bowing deeply, the long silk scarf covering Samuel's injured face caught on his shoe. When he stood upright, the caught scarf pulled off his face.

To our great surprise, the actor playing Juliet was not Samuel.

It was Judith.

CHAPTER EIGHT

"Oh no," said Anne, looking at me with terror in her eyes.

"It will be all right," I tried to reassure her. "No one will notice."

Judith reattached the silk scarf to cover her face, and Richard took her arm to usher her off stage. For a moment, I thought no one had noticed. And then, a loud voice echoed across the Great Hall.

"Witch!"

The crowd fell silent. Judith stopped walking and froze for a moment. Richard paused, and he then stood in front of Judith and addressed the crowd.

"Thank you all for coming to tonight's performance!" he bowed low as the crowd began to murmur.

"She's a witch!"

"There are no witches here," said Richard. "I can assure you of that. Only skilled actors playing their parts a little too well. Nothing but the best for His Majesty!"

"Make Juliet remove her scarf," came a voice.

Another said, "Take off your scarf!"

The same people who moments before were clapping enthusiastically now turned against Judith and Richard. The crowd began chanting, "Witch! Witch! Witch!" Richard and Judith tried to exit the stage, but guards stopped them.

An old woman darted forward and pulled the scarf from Judith's face. "See! She bares the mark of a witch!" She pointed to a mole on Judith's neck. "It's a sign of her pact with the Devil!"

"I saw her talking to a black cat in the courtyard!" came a voice.

"So did I!" said another.

Malachi Hunter came forward and addressed the crowd.

"My friends, this explains so much. We are gathered here to embark on our mission of purifying the Church. We have come to liberate it fully from the dark influences of Rome. It's only logical that the Devil and his followers should try to infiltrate this holy gathering. There is a witch among us. And where there is one witch, there are always more. Look around the room! Who else among us is a part of this evil coven, led by these malicious actors?"

"The herbalist!"

"And her two sisters!"

"Yes," said Malachi. "The weird sisters."

"I went to the herbalist for a boil I had," said a man. "She wanted to pierce it with a bodkin! She's a witch!"

"Do you still have the boil?" asked Malachi.

"Yes," said the man, pulling up his sleeve and revealing a nasty-looking boil.

"That proves it!" said a woman.

"Yes, that proves it!" echoed voices around the room.

"And it proves he is a witch, too!"

"Please!" came a voice, silencing the crowd.

It was Samuel Winston. His face was badly swollen. He walked to the center of the performance space, stood near Malachi, and faced the crowd.

"My name is Samuel Winston. I'm the actor hired to perform as Juliet tonight." He pointed towards Judith. "The only reason this young woman acted in the show tonight is because I could not."

"She bewitched him!" said someone in the crowd.

"Yes! Yes! She bewitched him!" rang out several voices. "She's a witch! This proves it!"

"No!" Samuel pointed to Malachi. "I couldn't perform because of this man. He struck me in the face so hard I was unable to be in tonight's show. Judith took my place at the last moment. She did it to help me. She did it for all of *you*!"

The crowd murmured.

"You dare accuse a man of the cloth?" Malachi said.

"It's true," said Oliver Fletcher, standing and addressing the crowd. "I'm a witness. Malachi Hunter grabbed the young woman who performed tonight, and Samuel Winston came to her aid. Malachi Hunter then hit Samuel in the face. We took him to the herbalist, and she applied a poultice to his face to help treat the swelling. But she told us that there was no way that he would be in the condition to perform tonight."

"So, the herbalist bewitched them both!"

"Yes," said a middle-aged woman. "Last winter I called the herbalist to help me give birth, but the baby was stillborn. She's a witch! She killed my baby!" The woman began sobbing uncontrollably.

Malachi held up his hands to silence the crowd. "This man claims to be an Anglican priest. But is he really? Perhaps he is actually the high priest of a witches' coven. Who else would come so quick to the aid of a known witch?"

"Yes!" voices shouted. "He is the witches' high priest!"

"Or even worse," said a tall man with sunken features. "He is secretly a Roman Catholic."

"Let's not get sidetracked from the issue at hand," said Thomas Winter. His brother Robert and a few others were standing with him. "The issue here is not Catholicism, but witchcraft."

"Please," said Samuel. "None of these people have done anything wrong. You're letting your fears overtake you. This is simply a misunderstanding."

The people murmured. I had seen crowds behave this way before. They are fickle by nature and easily swayed. I had a glimmer of hope that we could avoid this impending tragedy. And then someone asked him, "Where are you from, sir?"

"I'm from Bristol," said Samuel.

"Now I know where I've seen him before," said Sarah Goody. The crowd fell silent as she walked up and looked at Samuel. "From Bristol, are you?"

"Yes, my lady," he responded.

"And you're from the Winston family?"

"Yes, ma'am." Samuel seemed very nervous.

Lady Goody turned and faced the crowd. "Ladies and gentlemen, I happen to know the Winston family from Bristol. They are, in fact, well-known in Bristol. For the terrible plague that haunts our land so mercilessly began at their neighbor's home."

The crowd gasped. I looked at King James who was sitting on the edge of his seat. He looked intense and concerned. I wished that I knew what he was thinking.

"I also know that the Winston family doesn't have a son," Lady Goody continued. "Not one named Samuel, or otherwise. In fact, they have only one daughter. And her name is Samantha." She looked at Samuel accusingly. "Sir," she said. "If I use that term correctly. Please remove your hat."

"Remove your hat!" demanded the crowd. "Take off your hat!"

"This is ridiculous," said Samuel. "I will do no such thing."

He turned to leave, but armed guards stopped him.

"Sir," said a guard. "Take off your hat."

"Take off your hat!" yelled someone in the crowd. "Only a witch would defend a witch!"

"That's right!" said Malachi. "Only a witch would defend a witch."

The crowd began chanting, "Only a witch would defend a witch! Only a witch would defend a witch!"

Malachi walked over to Samuel and pulled the hat from his head. A guard then forced Samuel to his knees, grabbed his hair, and pulled the ties from it. Beautiful long hair came cascading down. The crowd gasped.

"It's true!" said Malachi. "This 'man' is actually a woman, pretending to be a man."

"Witch!" said someone in the crowd. "A woman should not wear the clothes of a man!"

"Both girls were walking around the palace together all day," said an old man.

"And they both petted a black cat outside," said another.

"Everyone pets that little cat," said a young woman.

An old woman grabbed her arm and shouted in her face, "Only a witch would defend a witch!"

The young woman looked terrified. "That's what I mean! Clearly anyone who petted that cat is a witch. I never would, that's for sure! They *are* witches, that's my point!"

"I saw them in Gallery Hall today," said another young woman. "They must have conjured up the ghost!"

"The ghost!" people exclaimed. "They're conjuring up ghosts to haunt the palace!"

"The plague began at her neighbor's house," said Lady Goody. "And it spread from there. But she never caught it. Thousands are dead, but she lives."

"Thou shalt not suffer a witch to live," hissed Malachi.

"They are in league with the Devil," said a guard. "And with each other."

"Arrest them!" demanded the mob. "Burn them! Put an end to the plague!"

"Yes, the plague," said Malachi. "Who among us hasn't lost someone to the plague? Raise your hand if it hasn't taken someone you love?"

No one raised a single hand.

"Come now," said Malachi. "Surely there is at least one among us whom the plague hasn't touched."

"The black death has stung all of us," said a toothless old man. "Every one of us has lost loved ones."

"Well," Malachi said with a wicked smile. "Here stands before you the cause of all their suffering. Here stands the source of all our pain. Here stands the root of England's downfall. Our path is clear. *Thou shalt not suffer a witch to live!*"

The mob chanted: "Thou shalt not suffer a witch to live! Thou shalt not suffer a witch to live!"

I had to intervene. I ran to the stage area and raised my hand to silence the crowd. They ignored me, and continued chanting, "Thou shalt not suffer a witch to live! Thou shalt not suffer a witch to live!" After a few moments, someone shouted, "Let the king's witchfinder speak!" It was the court physician, William Butler. The crowd calmed, but only a little.

"Friends, Englishmen, fellow Christians," I spoke aloud. "Listen to me, I implore you. As Malachi has so rightly spoken, we have all lost loved ones to the plague. And Malachi is a good Christian man."

"Yes," someone agreed. "A good Puritan, he is!"

"No one wants to see justice done more than I," I said. "But if the arrow of justice is to hit its mark, one must aim it at the proper target."

The crowd became quiet.

"I am here to be the watchdog of your anger. I am here to assure that your arrow flies true. Of this I can promise you: When someone contracted the plague, none wept harder than these two. When someone was sick, they helped them. When someone cried, they consoled them. When someone died, they buried them. Does this sound like the actions of a witch?"

The crowd murmured. I raised my hand again, and they became silent.

"But Malachi says they are witches," I continued. "And Malachi is a *good* Christian man."

"Malachi hit a woman," said a man in his early thirties. "What kind of man hits a defenseless woman?"

"That's right," said a young woman standing next to him. "Only a coward hits a woman."

"Please," I said to the crowd. "I do not judge Malachi. That is not my place. I stand before you today, and I affirm that Malachi is a good Christian," I paused ever so briefly, "*man*."

"Hit a poor little girl, did you? Make you feel like a big man, did it?" said a strong-looking man in his early forties. "I've half a mind to show you what a good fist to the face feels like, you coward."

"Please," I implored the crowd. "There is only one of us here who has the authority to be the judge, juror, or executioner of these women." I gestured to Malachi. "Or of this man." I bowed before King James. "And that is His Majesty, the king. A man of whom I can personally testify is truly a good Christian man." I began applauding, "Let's hear it for the king!"

The crowd applauded wildly. There were several whistles, and everyone was on their feet and clapping for the new king. The king stood, smiling, drinking in the applause. He let the cheering go on for several moments. Finally, he raised his hand to quiet the crowd.

"Please, you are too kind," said King James. "The Lord has called me to be humble, and I'm very proud of that." He turned and looked at the accused. "Malachi is right, witchcraft is indeed the root of all our problems. And William is also right, we need to make sure we only execute actual witches. I have interrogated many witches in Scotland. We need a full and complete investigation first—that takes a day or two—*then* we will declare them guilty. Until that time, we shall proceed with caution."

For a moment, I felt relief. But then the king added, "Both Malachi and William will investigate this matter for me. Guards, arrest these two women, and for now, no one else. Put them in a bare and cold room, with no furniture and no fire. Hold them there as prisoners awaiting execution. Charge them with the crime of witchcraft."

The king walked to the center stage area and looked me in the eyes. "And I shall not release them until it is proven otherwise."

CHAPTER NINE

Judith's arrest haunted my thoughts as I walked down Gallery Hallway. My task was now much more complicated, and speed was even more important. My breath streamed through the bitter air like a ghost in a graveyard. Shivering, I crossed my arms over my chest. As I walked, I had a strange feeling that I was being watched. There was a sense of presence in the hallway. And then I heard something.

Thump.

I froze to the spot; there was only silence. After a few moments, I continued to walk down the hall. Then I heard it again.

Thump.

My heart beat wildly within me.

Thump.

"Is someone there?" I asked.

There was no response.

"What's going on here?" I demanded.

"Witchcraft," whispered a woman's voice.

"Show yourself at once," I ordered, trying to sound brave. "I am here on the king's authority."

Thump.

"Show yourself!"

Thump.

And then I saw it.

Down the hall from me, about twenty feet, there was *something*. At first, it appeared to be a mist gathering in the hallway. It spiraled around in a circle. The mist thickened and solidified, taking shape and form. It was a woman dressed in long robes. She had her back to me. My heart beat faster; my legs turned to lead.

"Hello?" I whispered with all the strength I could muster.

The figure was more substantial now. She turned her head towards me. Her long hair moved to one side revealing her cheek, pale like frozen moonlight. Her head continued to turn, and I knew I had to escape. Making the sign of the cross, I turned and ran the other way.

Thump, thump, thump!

She was coming after me; I didn't dare stop or turn around. I ran as fast as I could towards the nearest door.

Thump, thump, thump!

As soon as I reached the door, I turned the handle, but it was locked.

Thump, thump, thump!

Pounding on the door with my fists, I shouted for someone to let me in. Her freezing breath scorched the back of my neck, and her icy hand gripped my shoulder. I turned to face her. My eyes rose to meet her spectral gaze, and she said in a raspy voice, "Wake up, William, you're having a nightmare."

I awoke, and my wife Anne was shaking me.

"Are you okay?" she asked.

"Yes," I said, getting my bearings. The dream felt so real, it was hard to shake it off. Ghosts had always terrified me. That was why I used them in my plays. "I'm sorry I woke you, my dear."

"I couldn't sleep," said Anne, running her fingers through her long hair. "I'm so worried about Judith."

"So am I," I said, and looked out the window. "It's almost light."

"As soon as we can, I want to go visit Judith."

"We will." I started dressing for the day.

"William, what are we going to do?" Anne put on her dress and pulled her hair back.

"I will find the murderer," I said, combing my hair. "That will prove that Judith is innocent."

"Malachi Hunter will be hard to convince."

"We don't have to convince him," I said, opening the door. "We only have to convince King James."

"Judith's arrest changes everything," Anne said as she slipped on her shoes and stepped out into the hall with me.

"I know," I said, quieting my voice in the hallway. "I need to take my investigation in a new direction, and I have to find the killer as soon as possible."

We walked down the hall towards the room where they were keeping Judith and Samantha. We noticed Oliver Fletcher walking in front of us.

"Good morning, Father," I called. "Can we speak with you a moment?"

"Of course," said Fletcher. "I was going to see if they will let me visit the girls."

"So are we," said Anne. "We wanted to thank you for standing up for Judith."

"I wish I could have done more," he said.

We rounded the corner and saw the herbalist, Violet Lewis. She was speaking to the two men guarding the door to the makeshift jail cell.

"Please," Violet implored. "I need to apply fresh poultices to my patient's face."

"Is there a problem?" I asked a guard.

"No sir," he replied. "She can go in. As long as the king's Witchfinder vouches for her, my lord."

"I do," I said, feigning confidence.

"Wait," said the second guard. "Malachi Hunter ordered that no one visit the witches. He is a witchfinder, too."

"I override that order," I said firmly. "He is my assistant. I'm in charge of the investigation."

The two guards looked at each other.

"Never mind," I said, turning to walk away. "It's clear my time would be better spent rooting out witchcraft among the palace guards."

"Right this way, my lord." The first guard opened the door and let the four of us in. "And if there is anything else that I can do for you, please let me know."

The room was frigid, and there was very little light. The air was stale. I felt sorry that they imprisoned these young women, but I was thankful that the palace didn't have a dungeon. I looked at Samantha. She was clad in a simple dress and her hair was down on her shoulders. Seen in this way, I couldn't imagine we ever believed she was a boy.

Violet sat down her herb basket and inspected Samantha's face. "Are you in much pain?"

"No, miss," said Samantha. "I will be fine. It's the least of my problems."

Violet dabbed salve on Samantha's face. "You're healing nicely. You look like you'll be as good as new in a day or two."

"Yes," said Oliver, smiling. "You look radiant."

"Nonsense," she said. Even in the dim light, I could see that Samantha was blushing. She smiled and lowered her eyes. "You flatter me, my lord."

"I don't, my lady." Now it was Oliver's turn to blush. "I was concerned about you. I'm glad to know you're all right," he paused, smiled, and then added, "Samantha."

There was a brief silence, and then Judith said, "I'm fine, too."

Anne glanced at me and smiled for the first time since last night. She then said to Judith, "What can we do to help you?"

"Prove me innocent," she replied to her mother. Judith looked at me. "Or prove someone else guilty."

"I will, I promise you," I said, trying to reassure her with my smile.

"Yes, my dear," said Anne. "Try not to worry."

"I'm glad they didn't arrest you last night," I said to Violet.

"I am too, my lord," she replied.

"You're very brave to come here," said Anne.

"I have a duty to my patients." Violet gathered up her salves. "If I can keep someone from suffering even a little, I always do what I can."

"That's very noble," I said. "Did you learn herbalism from your mother?"

"Yes," said Violet. "She taught me many things."

"Does she work in the palace, too?" asked Anne.

"No, madam," Violet replied, her smile fading from her face. "She died a few years ago."

"I'm sorry," said Anne.

"Thank you," said Violet. "I'm grateful I still have my father and sisters. Although we don't always see eye to eye about everything."

"No family does," said Judith.

"Well, try to support them in any way you can," I said. "Even if you don't always agree."

"I will," said Violet.

"I admire you," said Judith, "and your work as a healer."

"Thank you, miss."

"Please," said our daughter, "call me Judith."

"And please call me Violet," she said in return. "It is my hope that I've made two new friends here today."

"That's our hope, too," said Samantha.

"I'd better go," I said, and knocked on the door to signal the guards to unlock it. "I promise I will get you both out of here."

"Me too," said my wife. "I will do anything to get you released."

We left the room, but Violet and Oliver stayed behind to comfort the girls. Anne said she needed to return to our room to rest and think. We said goodbye and parted.

I had to do something fast, but didn't know where to begin. My mind raced as I walked down the hall. Thoughts about the murder, my daughter's arrest, and witchcraft haunted me. I had to find Malachi and find out if we could have a reasonable conversation. We needed to work together now and solve this murder.

It was the first day of the conference. Hundreds of people were having breakfast in the Great Hall. Several people watched me as I entered, and whispered to each other. My new fame as the king's Witchfinder General had spread fast.

People crowded the room. There was a small table off to the side where one man was sitting, eating bread, and drinking hot tea. He had short brown hair, a mid-length beard with flecks of grey, and he dressed as a gentleman.

"Pardon me, sir," I bowed my head. "May I sit with you for breakfast?"

"Of course," he said, offering his hand to shake. "My name is Edward Wilkinson."

"Nice to meet you. I'm William Shakespeare."

"Oh yes, I know," he smiled. "The 'Witchfinder General.'"

"I'm afraid so," I said, sitting down and pouring a cup of hot tea.

"Have a roll of bread," said Edward, breaking a piece in half and handing it to me. There was honey on the table, and I drizzled it on my bread.

"How is witch hunting going?"

"I wish I knew where to start," I said, surprising myself with my openness.

"I was a sheriff and alderman at one time," he said, dripping honey onto his bread. "Before I lost my leg in Her Majesty's service."

He intrigued me. "In the war against Spain?"

"I fought in the war with Spain," he said, finishing his tea, "but I lost my leg in the Tyrone Rebellion." He shook his head. "We started the war by fighting with swords and we ended it by fighting with muskets. Say what you will about our new monarch, but I'm grateful that both wars ended when he became king."

My eyes drifted down to where his leg had been; his right leg was missing from the knee down. Catching myself, I looked up, embarrassed.

Edward laughed. "It's all right to look." He pulled his leg out and patted his thigh. "A musket ball shattered my shin. It could have been worse. My only regret is that my adventuring days are over. I especially miss being a sheriff. I loved investigating mysteries, solving crimes, and helping people."

"Tell me," I stopped eating and looked at him. "Have you ever investigated a murder?"

"Oh yes," he said. "Many times."

Hoping to learn something from him, I kept quiet and gave him my full attention. He poured another cup of tea.

"First, you need to interview suspects. Learn all you can from them. No fact is insignificant."

"That's what I've been doing," I said.

"Then you're on the right path. Also, gather as much information as you can. Treat everything as evidence. Look for clues everywhere."

As he spoke, I patted my pocket to find out if the vial was still there, and it was. The witch's poppet that started my adventure also came to mind. I wondered, *have I missed anything?*

"Develop an eye for detail. Use your mind. Apply the principles of logic and reason. But use your imagination, too."

He finished his tea, put a crutch under his right arm, and pulled himself up.

"Any other advice?" I asked, sorry that he was leaving.

"Yes," he said, as he put on his hat. "When you fail, and you will, abandon reason and follow your instincts. Your feelings are your thoughts working on a deeper level. Trust them."

We said goodbye, and I finished my bread. While I poured a last cup of tea, I saw my wife enter the Great Hall. Her face was white. I leapt up and ran to her.

"What's wrong, Anne? Are you all right?"

"Will," she said, breathing hard. "Someone was in our room and they went through all our things. They ripped everything apart!"

CHAPTER TEN

It surprised me how well someone had searched our room. Our clothes littered the floor. The pages of my manuscripts lay like autumn leaves on the ground. We began straightening up our small apartment.

"Look," said Anne. "They even ripped open our mattress."

While stuffing handfuls of feathers back into the mattress, I noticed something underneath the bed. I reached under and pulled out a small wax figure.

"What is it?" asked Anne.

"It's a witch's poppet."

"What's that?"

I looked up at Anne. "It's a little doll made to represent someone. It's used for casting spells on the person it represents." I looked closely at the wax figure. "It's holding something in its hand."

Anne inspected the doll. "It's a quill. Will, I think this represents you."

"Who would do this?" I wondered aloud.

"This means there truly are witches in the palace," said Anne, crossing herself.

"Do you think they're responsible for the assassination attempt?" I asked.

"Probably, but why would they want to kill the king?"

"Because of his witch hunting in Scotland." I said. "Hundreds were arrested, tortured, and killed there. A few years ago, there were a long series of investigations and persecutions. I would imagine that English witches don't want the same to happen here."

"Yes, right," said Anne. "I heard that in Scotland they pierced the skin of suspected witches with needles; I never understood why."

"They say witches have a 'Devil's mark' which prevents them from experiencing pain. Using needles to pierce them is a way of determining if they have the mark."

Anne shook her head. "I heard that in Scotland there are professional witch-prickers. I hope the king doesn't gift you with that title next."

"Me too."

"Will," said Anne, touching my arm. "You must be their target now that it's known you're the king's witchfinder."

"You're right," I said, nodding my head. I noticed something. "Look, there's something on the back of the door."

Anne walked over and removed a sheet of parchment that was hanging there. Someone had pinned it to the door with a silver dagger. Anne unfolded the paper, read it, and turned white.

"What does it say?"

She looked at me. "It says, 'Thou shalt not suffer a witch to live.'"

I clenched my fists. "Malachi."

***

I had to confront Malachi, but I needed a few minutes to calm down first. I was in a race against time, so I decide to return to the scene of the crime. When I reached the door of the chapel, the guard let me in without a single word. My new found fame had some advantages.

"Hello," said Father Talbot. "Here early for the noonday service?"

"No," I said. "I want to have another look around. Are you leading the noon prayers?"

"Fortunately, I don't have to," he said. "Now that Father Page is gone, I've been promoted." He looked proud. "Now I'm in charge of scheduling priests to officiate services. I only do the important ones now. No more Noonday Prayer services for me."

I shrugged. "It's all God's work."

"I suppose," said Talbot. "But I have my career to think about. The meek may inherit the earth, but they don't become bishops."

Not sure how to respond, I simply said, "Indeed."

"I'll call the sexton to assist you," said Talbot.

"Actually, I would rather talk to you if I may."

"As I said," he replied, "I've been promoted. I'll call the sexton to assist you." He turned and called out in a loud voice, "Alban!"

"Yes sir?" said Alban as he entered the nave from the sacristy.

"Please assist the Witchfinder General." Talbot turned and left the chapel with no further pleasantries.

"He seems happy with his new promotion," I said to Alban Braunstone.

"An ambitious man is never happy for long," said Alban. "There's always something more on the horizon." He paused, and then added, "If I may be so bold."

"I hope you know that you can speak candidly with me," I said.

"I'm an old man," Alban smiled. "I can speak candidly with anyone I want."

"Have you thought of anything that may help in my investigation?"

Alban scratched his beard. "This palace is filled with mysteries. Witchcraft, hauntings, and now murder. There are hundreds of rooms, and at times nearly a thousand people here. And there are even secret rooms and passageways."

"There are?"

"Yes," he replied. "They're unknown to most people here."

"Can you tell me where they are?"

"If I was a spry young fellow with the curiosity I had in my youth, I'm sure I would've rooted out all of them. But I'm too old to go adventuring. Nowadays I spend most of my free time reading books I've gathered and preserved over the years. I only know what I hear."

"And what do you hear?"

"That King Henry VIII had a secret room below the palace that has been walled off. I'm told you can still access it by the Silver Stick Stairs."

"Oh," I said. "I know where those stairs are."

"Good," he said. "It's said to be haunted by the ghost of Jane Seymour."

"One of King Henry's wives."

"Yes," Alban nodded. "Witnesses report that her spirit glides down the Silver Stick Stairs. They say she's dressed in a white gown and holding a candle."

"More ghost stories," I said.

"Quite." Alban smiled. "Still, I wouldn't want to go there at night and by myself if I were you."

I smiled back. "Any other advice?"

"Only this," said Alban. "Be careful of your fellow witch hunter."

"What do you mean?" I asked. I didn't trust Malachi at all, but it intrigued me that someone else shared my opinion.

Alban glanced around the room. Seeing it was empty, he leaned in and whispered, "The guiltiest are the quickest to condemn."

***

I searched for Malachi throughout the palace. I checked the Great Hall, the library, and even the royal tennis courts. I finally found him as he was coming out of the Great House of Easement, a grand name for the public lavatory, in the building to the right of the Main Gatehouse.

"Malachi," I said, holding back my anger. "We need to speak. Have you been in my room?"

"Of course not," said Malachi. "Why do you ask?"

"Someone has been in our room and has rummaged through all our things." I handed him the poppet. "And I found this under the bed."

Malachi looked at it for a moment and then dropped it to the floor. He glared at me with fire in his eyes. "A witch's poppet!" he yelled. "Did your daughter share your room before her arrest?"

"Of course."

"Then this proves she is a witch!" said Malachi. "She left behind evidence of her craft."

"The image on the poppet is of me," I said, trying to remain calm. "My daughter would never do that."

"You never know about witches," said Malachi. "They often fool even those closest to them. Especially if they're under a witch's spell."

"Nonsense," I replied. "Judith is not a witch."

"How can you be sure? You're new to witch hunting, but I worked for His Majesty before in this capacity. I served him in Scotland several years ago during the great witch hunt, although I never met him in person." Malachi smiled. "I don't mean to brag, but I was one of the torturers of

Margaret Aitken, the Great Witch of Balwearie. I know how to make a witch talk."

"I had no idea that you were such a celebrity," I said dryly.

"Oh yes." He missed my sarcasm. "Margaret Aitken confessed under torture and then made a deal to lead us to many witches throughout the land. In exchange for her life, of course."

"I would imagine she was motivated to do so."

"Yes," said Malachi, who seemed proud to tell of his part in the Scottish witch hunt. "And I was at the witch trial in Aberdeen against Janet Wishart and her collaborators."

"I'm not familiar with Janet Wishart," I said.

"No?" he seemed incredulous. "You call yourself a witchfinder, and you are ignorant of the Wishart witch?"

"I'm afraid so."

"She was a dreadful witch. Used spells to make it storm and bring sickness and fevers. She even used 'nightmare cats' to inflict horrifying dreams."

I remembered the little black cat in the courtyard, and the terrible dream I had the night before.

"There was so much evidence against her we had no trouble convicting her. She couldn't withstand my bodkin. I had to prick her thousands of times over a period of several days, but eventually she confessed. We proved in court that she was guilty, and she was hanged and then burned at the stake."

"And her entire family with her, I suppose."

Malachi shook his head. "Unfortunately, no. Her family was banished, but we convicted her son, Thomas. He was the ringleader, and in league with the Devil himself. He was executed, too."

"Gruesome work," I said, shaking my head.

"That's where you and I differ," said Malachi. "You don't have the stomach for this kind of work."

"I prefer the theater," I said.

"I used to love the theater," he said, "until I realized the error of my ways. When I was young, I acted in a traveling show. We traveled throughout England performing, and even up into Scotland. That's where I realized that theater was the Devil's work. There's nothing in the Bible about theater, so we shouldn't allow it. That's why I left the theater and trained to be a witch-pricker."

"That takes training? Don't you just stick a suspect with a pin at random until she confesses?"

"Bah," Malachi waved his hand as if he were waving away a foul smell. "That's what many fools think. No, you have to find the Devil's mark, a certain spot on a witch's body where you can insert a pin without pain or bleeding." He paused, and a wicked smile spread across his face. "Or at least with *little* pain or bleeding."

"You seem to relish the work." I said, disgusted. "Why did you leave Scotland?"

"After the witch trials that year died down, I came home to England to continue my work here," said Malachi. He paused and then looked at me with a penetrating stare. "Now I have a question for you. Have you inspected the body of the murdered priest for witch marks?"

"No," I said. "There is no body."

"What do you mean?"

"It disappeared from the doctor's examination room."

"Oh no," said Malachi, looking horrified. "Do you know what that means?"

"No, what?"

"They'll use it for their Black Mass."

"I don't understand."

"Witches have no creative power of their own. They only mimic and mock Christian rituals. They imitate the Mass, but twist it for their evil intent. They worship Lucifer rather than our Lord." He paused and looked at me without blinking. "And they'll use the murdered priest for their Unholy Communion."

Suddenly the full impact of what he was saying dawned on me.

"Cannibalism," I said, and made the sign of the cross.

CHAPTER ELEVEN

Although I hated it, I had to work with Malachi Hunter. It seemed to be the wisest course of action for the moment. If there is a wasp in the room, I want to know where it is. In other words, working with him would be the best way of keeping an eye on him and avoid getting surprised by his sting. Malachi went in search of the body, and I searched for secret rooms and passageways.

As I walked towards the Silver Stick Stairs, I passed by the kitchen. There was laughter coming from a side room used by the servants when they were off duty. Through the doorway, I noticed several servants, some of whom I recognized. There was the elderly couple, Alyce and Henry. Myles Lewis and his daughters, Elspet and Janet, were there, too. And a few others I had not yet met were also on break in the room.

"Come in, sir, come in," said Janet, smiling.

"I'm sorry," I said. "I don't want to intrude."

"Nonsense," said Elspet. "We'd love to chat with you for a while." She looked at Janet and smiled.

"Elspet," said Myles Lewis. "I'm sure His Majesty's Witchfinder General has more important things to do than socialize with servants. It's important work, rooting out witchcraft."

"What did he say?" Henry asked his wife, Alyce.

"He asked the gentleman which draft he would like," replied Alyce in a loud voice. She turned to me and said, "Nice cold draft of ale is what you're after, is it? We have several fresh ones to choose from."

"No, thank you."

"No need to be embarrassed, my lord," said Henry. "Why, I myself have been drinking heavily all morning."

"You have?" asked Myles in a stern voice.

"Have what?"

"Been drinking ale all morning," said Myles.

"What?"

"Drinking ale!"

"I'd love some," said Henry.

"Never mind," said Myles.

"What?" Henry asked in a loud voice.

Myles rolled his eyes. "I said, *never mind*!"

Henry shook his head. "Whisper and shout, whisper and shout, that's all people do anymore. I've worked in this palace for nearly fifty years; I remember when I was young, people spoke up in clear voices."

"Be that as it may," said Myles in a loud firm voice. "I will remind you that no job is permanent. Please respect the head servant."

"Oh, of course, of course," said Alyce. "You certainly have our respect, sir. 'Always respect your betters,' that's what I say." Alyce curtsied to Myles.

"That's better," said Myles as he turned back towards me.

"Wretch," said Alyce in what she seemed to think was a quiet voice.

Myles glanced at her, and she smiled innocently. It appeared as though he was going to address her malfeasance, but instead he just looked at me for sympathy and shook his head. I smiled at Myles.

"I'm sorry, sir," he said to me. "What can we do for you?"

"Nothing, thank you," I said, and turned to leave. Then I realized something. If Alyce and Henry had worked in the palace for so many decades, they may know of any secret passages or rooms. I thought it best to ask them in private.

"May I please speak to Alyce and Henry for a moment?"

"Of course," said Janet. "My sister and I have to get back to the bakery, anyway."

"That's right," said Myles, clapping his hands. "Everyone, back to work."

The servants filed out past me. Myles gave me a sympathetic glance as if to say, *good luck with them.*

When the room was clear, I moved closer to the elderly couple. I wanted to whisper, but I would have to speak louder than I thought prudent.

"Do you know where any secret passages are?" I asked, as loudly as I dared.

"What's that?" asked Alyce, almost shouting.

"Secret passages," I said a little louder. "Do you know where any are?"

"Secret *sausages*?" asked Alyce, puzzled. "We have plenty of sausages, but they aren't much of a secret."

"Not sausages," I said, and then repeated in a loud voice, "*Passages!*"

"Whisper and shout, whisper and shout," said Henry, shaking his head.

"No need to yell, my lord," said Alyce. "Yes, sir, there are secret passages and rooms in this palace. But I wouldn't go searching for them if I were you."

"Why not?"

"Because, sir," said Alyce. "They are guarded by ghosts and protected by witchcraft."

"Nevertheless," I said. "Please tell me where to find them."

"All I can tell you is to begin your search by tapping on the walls in the rooms," said Alyce. "When you hear a hollow sound, it means that there may be an entrance to a passageway."

"Thank you," I said, disappointed. There must be nearly a thousand rooms in the palace. I felt as though I had wasted my valuable time.

"Our pleasure," said Alyce, curtsying. "We have great respect for our betters, don't we Henry?"

"That's nice," said Henry.

As I was leaving the room, I heard Alyce say under her breath, "Wretch."

I glanced back; Alyce was smiling at me innocently.

***

While continuing on my way towards the Silver Stick Stairs, I noticed Thomas and Robert Winter sitting at a small table and talking quietly with each other. As I walked towards them, they stopped speaking and seemed to wait until I passed. Then they resumed their whispers. I remembered what Edward Wilkinson, the retired sheriff, told me about looking everywhere for clues and evidence. And so, I stopped and went back to talk with them.

"Pardon me," I said. "May I speak with you a moment?"

Both men looked at me with stern expressions, but didn't say a word. After an uncomfortable moment of silence, I forced myself to speak again, this time in a commanding tone.

"What business brings you to the palace?"

"Isn't supporting our new king reason enough?" asked Robert.

"You are loyal subjects?"

"Yes," said Thomas. He glanced at his brother.

"And you are here for the conference?"

"In a sense," said Robert.

"Which side do you support, Puritan or Anglican?"

The two brothers looked at each other, and then Thomas said, "I'm afraid we don't fit neatly into either category."

I wasn't sure why the brothers were being so cryptic, but I had no real reason to suspect them either. Time was of the essence, so I bid them farewell and continued on my way.

One of the many oddities of Hampton Court Palace is how it can seem so crowded and opulent one moment, and so quiet and gloomy the next. As I turned to go down a side hallway, the noise behind me faded. For the next few moments, the only sound was my footsteps. When I stopped to look at a painting, however, I heard footsteps behind me. I glanced back, but there was no one else in the hall. After continuing on my walk for a few more steps, I stopped again and listened. Sure enough, it sounded as if someone took another step. I felt the familiar clench of my stomach and fear rising from the core of my being. Something ancient and primal awoke within me—a fear that had kept my ancestors alive for centuries.

"It's nothing," I whispered.

My heart beat faster, and my breathing became quick.

"It's just my imagination."

I strained to listen over my pounding heart. After waiting several moments and hearing nothing, my breathing returned to normal.

"This is ridiculous," I mumbled.

When I walked on, a board creaked behind me. Freezing to the spot again, I listened.

Thump.

My heart was beating so loud it made it difficult to concentrate.

Thump.

It was coming from inside the wall to my right. I knocked once on the wall and listened. There was only silence. After several moments, I walked on. But after a few steps, I heard it again.

Thump.

There was a door on the right a few feet forward, very near where the sound was coming from. I reached into my boot and took out a small knife, inserted it into the lock, and jiggled it. The lock clicked and then opened. What I saw inside chilled me to my bones.

There was a ring of lit candles on the floor. The candles framed a large chalk circle, nine feet in diameter. Spreading from the center of the circle to the outer ring was a five-pointed star, and at the tip of each point of the star was a candle. I didn't know what it was, but it filled me with dread. I also noticed a familiar odor, the same smell from the physician's office and the haunted hallway. I looked around the room, which was bare except for a lectern standing at the head of the star. It had an open book on it. I read these words in the flickering candlelight:

Words of power, words of might,
Brightest day and darkest night,
In the circle and the ring,
Curse the crown and kill the king.

I closed the book and looked at the ancient leather cover. On it were the words, *A Book of Shadows.*

I picked it up for evidence. Then I realized something: the candles were lit, but no one else was in the small room. I had been in the hallway and didn't see anyone leave through the only door. I put the book back. On a hunch, I walked around the room knocking on the walls, listening as I knocked. *Tap, tap, tap.* I knocked high and low on the walls. *Tap, tap, tap.* I was almost ready to give up, but then I knocked at just the right spot.

Thump.

Chapter Twelve

Running my fingers along the wall where I had heard the hollow sound, I searched for an opening mechanism. After several minutes of trying, I felt a small metal latch along the seam of the corner. I gripped the latch tightly and pulled it downward; a narrow door in the wall opened. I grabbed a candle and looked inside.

There was a spiral staircase going down into the darkness. An icy wind rising from the gloom brought a sickly sweet scent to my nose; a scent which was now familiar. A faint sound rose from deep within the pitch black. The distant sound of chanting ascended on the frigid air, but it was unlike any I had ever heard.

Candle in hand, I stepped into the darkness, and began my decent. Besides the chanting, the sound of water dripping echoed in the stairwell. I could only see a few feet in front of me, and the air was freezing. The stench of mold mixing with the sweet scent tightened my stomach. With every step downward, the chanting became clearer. I paused and listened to the words, which repeated over and over:

Astarte, Isis, Diana,
Demeter, Hecate, Kali, Inanna.
Astarte, Isis, Diana,
Demeter, Hecate, Kali, Inanna.

I recognized some words as the names of pagan deities. Terror rose within me, and for a moment I thought of returning to safety. Judith and Samantha came to my mind, and the imperative to free them before

Malachi had them burned at the stake. I shuddered, said a quick prayer, and continued my decent into the darkness.

When I reached the ground floor, I stepped off the stairs. There was a *squeak* at my feet; I looked down as a rat scurried over my shoe. The chanting was louder now, and the odor more intense. Inching forward, step by step, I moved closer and closer to the sound of the chant.

Running my fingers along the wall, I touched a door handle. I opened the door and looked around the dark room by the light of my flickering candle. There was a table in the center of the room, with a small vial on it filled with white fluid. The bottle had the same foul stench as the last vial. I slipped it into my pocket and continued to explore the room. Hooded robes hung on metal hooks, and I noticed a collection of silver daggers in a display case. Other than that, the room was empty. I stepped back into the passageway and continued towards the sound of the chanting.

There was a haunting beauty to the incantation, almost spellbinding, as the voices blended together in perfect harmony:

Isis, Astarte, Diana,
Hecate, Demeter, Kali, Inanna.
Isis, Astarte, Diana,
Hecate, Demeter, Kali, Inanna.

"No," I whispered. "Stay focused."

Like Ulysses tied to the mast of his ship, I fought the pull of the Sirens' song. I took a few deep breaths, and calmed myself.

The chanting continued, and with all the courage I could muster, I moved closer to the sound. Running my fingers along the dark wall as I walked, I found another doorway. I stepped inside. There was a tall figure standing in the center of the room. Startled, I dropped my candle. Scrambling to retrieve it, I gazed up at the towering figure. It was a man from the waist up, but it had the legs of a goat. Two horns were on its head. I reached out and touched the figure in front of me. To my relief, my fingers grazed the cold stone of a statue. Nothing else was in the room, so I continued down the hall towards the chanting.

A large wooden chest was sitting against the wall of the passageway. It had a lock on it, so I took out my boot knife and tinkered with the lock.

After a few moments of work, it clicked and unlocked. The box was filled with human bones. On the bones were strange markings carved deep into the surface. The thought of whose bones they were and how they got there made me shudder. I took another deep breath to settle my nerves. As I exhaled a white fog into the dim light of the candle, I closed the trunk and moved on. The chanting was louder than ever.

The light from my flickering candle revealed a wall ahead. I moved to the wall and placed my hand against it; I could feel the vibrations of the witches' chant. There seemed to be a power behind the wall, thrumming, resonating, and almost living.

Suddenly, the chant stopped, and I withdrew my hand. Then the voices spoke:

> *Double, double, toil and trouble;*
> *Fire burn and cauldron bubble.*
> *Cool it with a baboon's blood.*
> *Then the charm is firm and good.*

At that moment, an icy wind rose from somewhere in that dark lair, snuffing out my candle. Alone in the pitch dark, lost in that underground world, I realized that no one even knew I was there. Images of Anne, Judith, and Susanna came to my mind. I began to grope my way along the wall, back the way I had come.

Using the wall as a guide to keep from getting lost, I threaded my way through the dark. After a few moments, my shin bumped hard into another wooden trunk. I pulled the knife out of my boot, and began working the lock. It was my hope that there would be flint and steel inside the chest, so I kept turning my knife. The lock was stubborn, but it finally opened.

My fingers searched inside the box, and after a moment I touched velvet. The soft fabric was wrapping something solid, a few inches wide and almost a foot tall. I unwrapped the item and explored it with my fingers. It reminded me of a prop of a human skull that we used in a play once. My stomach turned when I realized that this was not a prop. Revolted, I put it back and closed the lid to avoid leaving evidence that I had been there. I stood up and continued retracing my steps back to the spiral staircase.

After progressing well for several minutes, I stopped to catch my breath. It was then that I heard something terrifying—a sound of scraping against the floor. There was *something* in the dark with me, but I didn't know what. And it was coming towards me.

"Who's there?"

The scraping continued, sounding like something dragging across the floor, coming closer towards me.

"Stay back."

Now the sound was only a few feet away from me.

"I'm warning you," I said. "I'm armed."

I turned to run, but tripped and slammed hard onto the ground. Something had caught my stocking. Pulling hard and kicking wildly, I scrambled to get free. Whatever had me wouldn't let go. With all my strength, I gave one mighty kick, freeing my leg. I reached down and felt blood seeping through my torn stocking; my leg had been caught on a metal spike. Breathing a sigh of relief, I stood up and listened. Whatever was causing the scraping sound was still coming towards me.

Inching my way back towards the spiral staircase, I moved as fast as I could, shuffling my feet to avoid tripping again. The dragging sound continued coming after me, along with the sound of heavy breathing.

To my great relief, my fingers grasped the cold metal rail of the staircase. A faint hint of light shone at the top of the stairs. It emanated from the open door in the room that first led me to this foul place. Relieved, I hurried up the stairs, never taking my eyes off the hopeful light shining through the dark above me.

Behind me, I could hear *whatever it was* climbing the stairs, step by step.

When I reached the top of the stairs, I stepped into the safety of the occult room that before had so terrified me. I slammed the secret door shut behind me and heard the latch click tight. My back pressed against the door, I slid down to the floor, breathing hard. Putting my head in my hands, I only then realized that I was shaking all over. I looked down at my torn stocking; there was blood staining the cloth where the spike had caught my flesh. I was glad to be back safe and alive.

But my relief was short-lived. At the door of the room were two guards, standing on each side of Malachi Hunter.

"William Shakespeare," Malachi spoke in a commanding voice. "By the power invested in me by His Majesty the King, I hereby arrest you for the high crime of witchcraft. And may God have mercy on your soul."

CHAPTER THIRTEEN

"Malachi," I said. "I'm glad you're here, I found—"

A guard punched me in the stomach; I doubled over in pain and fell to the floor. "Shut up, witch," the guard said, and kicked me in the side.

"Stop," said Malachi. "There is no need for that. He needs to be in good shape when we burn him at the stake for witchcraft." He knelt down near my ear and added, "And his daughter with him."

The two guards pulled me to my feet and dragged me out of the room.

"The king is in the Great Hall," said Malachi. "Take him there."

Struggling to breathe, nausea filled my stomach as I stumbled down the hallway with them. We entered the Great Hall; hundreds of people were there finishing their supper. The sound of conversation and laughter filled the air; I could smell roasted lamb and fresh-baked bread. The king sat at the royal table near the front of the dining room, finished with his evening meal.

Malachi strode to the front. "Your Majesty," he said in a loud voice, and the Great Hall became silent. "You have appointed me to investigate witchcraft at Hampton Court Palace, and I am honored to tell you that my search has been fruitful. By the authority invested in me by God and the Crown, I hereby accuse William Shakespeare of the high crime of witchcraft."

The guards flung me to the floor in front of the king. He looked shocked and stared hard at me for a moment. Catching my breath, I stood to face him.

"What's the meaning of this?" the king asked Malachi. "I personally picked this man to be our Witchfinder General."

"He fooled all of us, my lord," said Malachi. "Or at least most of us."

"What evidence do you have?" asked the king. "I demand answers."

"Your Majesty, these two noble palace guards and I caught William Shakespeare in the act of practicing black magic."

"Is this true?" the king asked the guards.

"Yes, sire," said the guard who had hit me.

"Or at least," said the other guard, "we found him in a room with cursed items."

"And where are these 'cursed items' now?"

"Here, Your Majesty." Malachi held up the book I had found in the room. "It's a witch's book of spells." Malachi turned and faced the crowd, holding up the book for all to see.

"A Book of Shadows," said the king, stroking his beard.

"Yes," said Malachi. "And there was a pentagram on the floor surrounded by candles."

"Witch!" a voice in the crowd bellowed.

"Sorcerer!" screamed another.

"Quiet!" said the king. He then turned to me. "How do you defend yourself?"

"Sire," I replied. "While investigating on your behalf, I found the room that Malachi described. I discovered the spell book and pentagram there."

The king nodded. "Is there any other evidence against this man?"

"Yes," said Malachi. "Your Majesty, I call as a witness the chief servant, Myles Lewis."

Myles Lewis was standing in back and looked shocked to hear his name. Malachi waved for him to come forward. Myles straightened his serving jacket and walked to the front.

"Yes sir," said Myles to Malachi.

"Tell the king what you found," said Malachi.

"Found, sir?"

"Don't play games with us," demanded Malachi. "I order you to testify to this court."

Myles looked at me and said, "I'm sorry, sir."

"Sorry for what?" I asked.

"Your Majesty," Myles said to King James. "Malachi Hunter ordered me to go into Master Shakespeare's room and search for evidence of witchcraft."

"And what did you find there?" asked the king.

"This is awkward, Your Majesty," said Myles.

"I understand," said the king, "but please continue."

"Forgive me, sir," Myles said to me.

"You will address the king and not the criminal," ordered Malachi.

Myles cleared his throat. "I found several items of witchcraft, such as a wand, pentacle, and an athame."

"What's an athame?" I asked.

"A ceremonial blade used by witches," said the king.

"Yes sire, and also a boline," said Myles. He then looked at me and gave a definition, "Another witch blade, a white-handled knife with a curved blade shaped like a crescent moon."

"But you missed an important piece of evidence," said Malachi. "Shakespeare himself showed me a witch's poppet that he had in his room."

"Why would he show that to you if he is a witch?" asked the king.

Malachi laughed. "He claimed that he found it in his own room. And with a stroke of evil genius, he even made the poppet to look like him. But I could not be so easily fooled."

"Of course," said King James. "Is that all?"

"No," said Malachi. "There is one more thing, Your Highness."

"Yes?"

Malachi reached into his pocket, pulled out a necklace with a star-shaped pendant, and showed it to the crowd. "A witch's pendant."

The crowd gasped and began murmuring.

"Where did you get that?" asked the king.

Malachi looked at me and smiled. "I took it off of William Shakespeare myself when we arrested him."

"You liar!" I said and sprang towards him, but the guards caught me and held me tight.

"A witch's amulet!" screamed a young woman.

"That proves it!" said an older man. "The king's witchfinder is a witch himself!"

"He's a witch!" said voices in the crowd.

"Silence!" King James stood and raised his right hand to quiet the crowd. "This is terrible news, my friends. I had no idea that witchcraft had climbed so high in the royal palace. I am afraid I am left with no choice but to deal with this crime with extreme prejudice."

The king stroked his beard for a moment and looked at me. Then he spoke out in a loud voice.

"William Shakespeare, you are hereby convicted of the high crime of witchcraft. The penalty is death by burning. You and your daughter shall be burned at the stake, and Samantha Winston shall be burned with you."

"The end of witchcraft!" shouted a tall man with a long red beard.

"The end of the plague!" said another voice from the crowd. "Hooray!"

"Seize him!" ordered Malachi. Two guards stepped forward and grabbed me by my arms.

A woman's laughter rang out across the Great Hall, silencing the crowd.

I turned my head towards the wicked laughter, and my blood ran cold. To my great surprise I saw my wife, Anne Hathaway. Clad in a long black gown, her hair flowed behind her as she strode forward from the back of the room. Her eyes were framed in dark; her face pale—almost white—her lips ruby red and twisted into a wicked smile. Taking center stage, she turned and addressed the crowd.

"Fools!" she shrieked. "You fumble around the palace and the countryside looking for witches to burn. You see sorcerers in every shadow, and magicians behind every curtain. And all the while the queen of all witches is right here among you."

I glanced at Malachi Hunter, who was staring at Anne in horror. She had everyone's attention, including mine.

"Wax figures and silver daggers are children's toys. Pentagrams and candles are meaningless in and of themselves. A real witch has no need of such playthings when the power of all existence courses through her veins."

She turned and glared at me. "William Shakespeare is not a witch. He could never master the witches' art, even if he wanted to." A wicked smile spread across her face. "For my amusement, I toyed with the Witchfinder

General like a cat with a mouse. While he was out hunting witches, I possessed his wife and stole her identity."

The crowd gasped and shouts of "No!" rang out across the Great Hall.

"It's true!" she continued. "I have been playing the role of Anne Hathaway, loyal wife and mother, and he was too stupid to even notice. I explored the palace and made my plans, and the king's Witchfinder never caught on."

She looked at King James, his eyes wide with shock.

"It is in Hampton Court Palace that I shall sit on my throne. I will rule over all Britannia, as witches did in the days of old. I am not some poor old widow tortured until she confesses to crimes she couldn't fathom. I am not a kind midwife whose only crime is to help women bear children. Fools! They are not witches!"

Anne threw back her head and let out a sinister cackle. I glanced at the crowd, and everyone was on their feet, transfixed on Anne.

"Judith and Samantha are only senseless children who love theater," she continued. "They have no magical power and no interest in the occult. They are just silly girls obsessed with games and dances and pretty dresses. Bah! It sickens me they would ever be accused of being something as grand as a genuine witch. Their arrest bears witness to the foolishness of the Crown."

The king looked indignant, and one of his guards looked to him for an order. King James glanced at him and shook his head.

"I am ancient," said the witch. "I have lived for thousands of years, and I shall live thousands of years more. I am birthless and I am deathless. I am known by many names."

She walked closer to the crowd, and several people shrank back.

"I was Lilith in the Garden of Eden. King Saul knew me as the Witch of Endor. King Arthur called me Morgan le Fey. And I have had many other names. Today, you may call me Ravynna the Witch, Queen of England."

Palace guards rushed the stage, swords drawn and muskets aimed at the witch. Anne Hathaway—*Ravynna*—raised her hand, and they stopped in their tracks.

"Fools!" she screeched. "Do you still not understand the power of a genuine witch? I have no need of swords and muskets to fight my battles.

I need no magic wands or wax poppets to kill my enemies. If I wanted to turn you to stone, I would simply blink my eyes."

Voices in the crowd cried out, but the guards stood their ground.

"If I wanted to burn you alive, I would utter a single magic word. If I snapped my fingers," she held her fingers as if she was going to do so, "you would turn to dust."

The guards began backing away from her.

"And if I wanted to kill the king," she looked at King James. The witch outstretched her fingers as if she was going to squeeze her hand tight. "All I would have to do is make a fist and he would burst into flames."

The king bravely met her gazed and never blinked. If he was afraid, he showed no signs of it. After a long moment, Ravynna the Witch smiled and turned away.

"Today I will let your petty king live, for he may prove useful to me yet." She looked at the king sternly. "But be warned, King James, that you serve at my pleasure. You live and you die at my command."

She turned away from him sharply and addressed the crowd. "And to all of you, know this: Ravynna sees all. Ravynna knows all. There are no whispers so quiet that I cannot hear them. There is no room in the palace so private that I cannot see into it. All of your actions, all of your words, and even all of your *thoughts*, are known to Ravynna the Witch."

The crowd stood in stunned silence. No one dared to speak or even move. After a long moment, Malachi Hunter moved to the witch's side. He looked at her for a moment and then knelt before her. He then stood and addressed the crowd in a loud voice.

"Long live Ravynna the Witch!"

Many in the crowd repeated after him, quietly at first, "Long live Ravynna the Witch."

Malachi said again, "Long live Ravynna the Witch!"

The entire crowd began chanting repeatedly, growing in intensity each time:

"Long live Ravynna the Witch."

"Long live Ravynna the Witch!"

"LONG LIVE RAVYNNA THE WITCH!"

Chapter Fourteen

Applause for Ravynna filled the Great Hall as she strode regally towards the door. She walked down the center of the crowd, and people parted before her like the Red Sea before Moses. They knelt before her as she passed them, and an old woman reached out for her hand and kissed it.

Stunned, I turned to the king. "Am I free to go?"

"Yes," said the king. "Return to your investigations. You have a killer to catch before he strikes again."

He then turned to a guard. "And release the two young women, too. Any fool can see that they're not real witches."

King James looked at me without blinking. "Not like Ravynna the Witch."

"Thank you, Your Majesty," I said. Relieved, I bowed before the king. He seemed not to notice and left the room with his entourage.

It was now dark outside; the day had passed so fast with all that had happened. Malachi Hunter walked up to me and spoke.

"You're a lucky man," he said.

"How so?"

"Being so close to Ravynna the Witch," he replied. "I've always been a huge supporter of witches, you know."

"You were a witch-pricker!"

"Yes, yes," he said, and then he added in a voice loud enough for anyone listening to hear, "but only *false* witches. My mission was to reveal all the fakers *pretending* to be real witches. Only those so bold as to try to steal the glory from the one true witch, our good Queen Ravynna."

"That's not the impression you gave earlier."

"Nonsense," said Malachi. "My historic support of witchcraft is well documented."

"Mine too," said a man next to me in a frightened voice.

"Mine too!" parroted several others, their words laced with fear.

A minstrel strummed his lute. "I'm inspired by Ravynna the Witch to compose a ballad in her honor."

"And I will create marvelous paintings of Her Majesty for Gallery Hall," said an artist.

"And sculptures of her for the Chapel Royal!" added another.

"Ravynna will save us," said an old woman, her eyes wide with terror.

"Ravynna will stop the plague," said an old man standing next to her.

"Mommy," a little girl tugged on her mother's dress. "I want to ask you something, but I don't know how to say it."

"Think of Ravynna and the words will come," said her mother.

The little girl closed her eyes and took a deep breath. "Can I be a beautiful witch queen when I grow up?"

"If Ravynna wills it, you will be," replied her mother, patting her on the head. "All hail Ravynna the Witch!"

"All hail Ravynna the Witch!" replied the little girl.

There was horror behind their words, but no one dared speak of it openly for fear that the witch may be listening. The crowd was dispersing when I noticed Alban Braunstone sitting at a small table near the back of the room. He looked at me and smiled sympathetically.

"William, are you all right?" he asked as I walked up to his table.

"My ribs are sore," I said. "But they don't seem to be broken."

"Still, you should visit the physician in the morning," he said. "But I was actually inquiring about your soul. How are you feeling about all this?"

"I don't know," I said, shaking my head. "I'm still in a state of shock. I'm exhausted, and there is so much to think about."

Alban stood up. "Will, get some sleep. If you need to talk, come see me in the morning."

"Thank you, I will," I said. "Should I meet you at the sacristy?"

"No," he replied, handing me a piece of paper with directions to his room written on it. "Too many ears there. Come to my room."

"Ravynna can see into all rooms, no matter how private."

Alban smiled. "Will, I am an old man. I have no fear of anyone at this point. Not kings and not witches. It will just be easier to talk openly in private. See you in the morning."

Tears for my wife running down my cheeks, I made my way back to my room and collapsed onto the ripped mattress. Exhausted, I fell asleep immediately, and dreamed about ghosts, bonfires, and Ravynna the Witch.

***

The bright sunlight shone into my room, warming my face as I awoke. I looked out the window at the icy gardens and thought about all that had happened the day before. I stepped out into the hall, and made my way towards Alban's room. Lost in my thoughts, it surprised me when someone grabbed my arm and whirled me around. It was Judith.

"Daddy!" she cried as she hugged me tight. "They released us this morning!"

"I'm so glad," I said, hugging her back, my eyes wet with tears. "Did they tell you why?"

Judith looked serious. "They said mother's a witch."

"She's not just a regular witch," said a servant girl who overhead us talking. With eyes filled with dread, she said in a loud voice, "She is the Witch Queen, ruler of England, Ireland, Scotland, and Wales. Long live Ravynna the Witch!"

"Long live Ravynna the Witch!" echoed the boy next to her as they walked on.

"Father, I don't understand."

"I know," I said. "Judith, I'm so sorry, but I need to go see someone. Rest, and we'll talk later."

Judith looked disappointed, but agreed. We hugged again and parted.

As I continued to make my way towards Alban's room, everyone I passed spoke about Ravynna with glowing words. I learned she had commandeered a luxurious private room, posted guards outside, and ordered that she not be disturbed.

When I got to Alban's room, he greeted me at his doorway and invited me in. His room was small and tidy. He had a simple bed and a small table with two wooden chairs. Books, scrolls, and manuscripts lined his walls, many appearing ancient. I would have loved to go through each one and explore the literary treasures he had amassed over the decades of his interesting life. However, we had more pressing matters to attend to. He offered me a seat and poured me a cup of tea.

"I see your eyes coveting my books," he said with a smile, taking a seat next to me.

"Yes," I said. "How did you gather so many ancient scrolls and manuscripts?"

"I worked in the monastery library," he said. "When Henry VIII dissolved the monasteries, I preserved as many as I could. Others I gained here and there through my various jobs, usually during a wave of persecution. A few were given to me right before their owners were arrested, hanged, or burned at the stake."

"They must be worth a fortune."

He nodded his head. "Historically, they're priceless. But I'm afraid they will be burned when found, and lost forever."

"Some are heretical?"

"Depending on who is in power at the moment, yes."

"Do you have any magical texts?" I asked.

He looked at me cautiously. "I've encountered magical teachings over my many years, yes. Of course, I studied it as a scholar and not as a practitioner."

"Alban," I said. "There are forces at work in this palace beyond my comprehension. Could you please teach me the basic principles of magic?"

He rubbed his eyes, took a deep breath, and let it out. "What would you like to know?"

I shrugged, not even knowing enough to ask an intelligent question. "What *is* magic?"

"Magic is the science of the occult. It seeks to harness and use *mana*, the underlying power latent in all creation. The magician taps into this universal spiritual force that permeates the entire universe. Through properly applying magical principles, practitioners direct this magic power to achieve their desired results."

Alban poured himself a cup of tea. He took a sip and continued.

"The most basic principle is, 'As above, so below.' Magic users believe that there are two worlds: the natural world here below and the supernatural world above us. By making a physical form of something, they believe that the higher spiritual world will bring about the desired effect on earthly matter."

"Like a witch's poppet."

"Yes," said Alban. "They mold and shape physical wax to represent a person. Then the supernatural world works to bring harm to the person who the wax represents."

"You're saying if one thing resembles another thing, they are connected magically?"

Alban nodded. "According to magic users, yes. And they believe this is especially powerful through *contagion*. In other words, once this item has been in physical contact with a person, that connection remains. This is true even if the victim becomes far removed from the cursed item. For example, a witch might stick a poppet with pins or throw it into the fire. This would harm or even kill the victim, even if he was far away."

"Perhaps that's why someone placed a poppet under my bed."

"Yes, I would think so," said Alban, taking a sip of tea. "And it may interest you to learn that magicians use a type of theater for magical purposes."

"How so?"

"A sorcerer might use his magic wand as a sword and act out thrusting it into his victim. He would try to add emotion and perform as though he were actually stabbing the person. Or a coven of witches might perform a ritual and act out all the parts of the situation they were trying to bring to pass. They would chant. Maybe use incense. Whatever they need to create a mystical atmosphere and bring their desires to life."

The chanting I had heard the day before came to mind. "So, to kill a king they would act out the king's death, with someone playing the part of the king?"

"Yes, that would be one way," said Alban.

"And does all this work?"

"Like I said, I am a scholar, not a practitioner."

"But you must have an opinion on the matter."

Alban shrugged. "I think the real 'magic' is the power of belief. If you believe strongly enough in something, it becomes true. Truth *happens*. It's a process. There is a Supreme Power in the universe that responds to our belief in it."

"So, if you really *believe* that a witch's poppet has power over you, then you may actually become sick if you know that the wax figure is being tortured?"

"Yes," said Alban. "You may even die from your negative belief, even if what you believe is not objectively true. Through the power of faith, it is still true *for you*."

"Belief is the key," I said, stroking my beard. "Faith is the real magic."

"Yes," said Alban. "In fact, many magicians and sorcerers try to manufacture people's faith in them by performing tricks to fool them into belief."

"Like what?"

"Oh, perhaps predicting the future, or describing things that only the victim would know. But it's all a trick. At least, in my humble opinion."

"Fascinating," I said. "Could the principle of belief also be used for good?"

"Yes," said Alban. "Believe that you will be successful and you will be. Have faith that your children will turn out well and it will come to pass. Believe that things will ultimately work out for the best, and they will. But believe that you are defeated, and you already are. Think you have a sickness, and you become sick. As you believe, so is it."

I shook my head. "So, a witch doesn't understand this deeper principle, but believes the poppet itself and surrounding rituals have power to make their evil wishes come true."

"That's right," said Alban. "At least, that's what I think."

"Actors know this to be true," I said. "To be authentic on stage, you need to believe you *are* the character you're portraying."

Alban nodded his head.

"Thank you, Alban." I stood and hurried to the door. "You have been very helpful."

"Where are you going?" asked Alban.

I turned back and smiled at Alban. "To see a witch."

CHAPTER FIFTEEN

Soon after leaving Alban's room, a sharp pain tore through my side. Leaning against the hallway wall, I cradled my aching ribs. In my imagination, I pictured a witch's bony fingers stabbing a wax poppet made in my image. I wasn't far from Doctor Butler's examination room, so I shook off my fears and walked in that direction. I rounded a corner and ran into Richard Burbage.

"Will," he said. "I've been looking everywhere for you. Are you all right?"

"Yes," I said, smiling through the pain. "But I'm going to visit the doctor just in case."

"Let me walk with you," he said, taking my arm.

"Thank you," I said. "I would like to talk with you."

"Will, please know that I had no idea Judith was playing Juliet until we were onstage. We didn't talk beforehand, and I assumed it was Samuel." He paused. "I mean Samantha."

"No need to apologize," I said. "I should have expected this." I smiled. "On a positive note, she is a great actor."

"Yes, it's in her blood." Richard let go of my arm. "Have you found the murdered priest's body?"

I shook my head. "Malachi Hunter said that the witches probably used it for their unholy communion."

"Perhaps," said Richard. "But I have little faith in the words of Malachi Hunter. He wears his soul on his face."

Stabbed by another pain, I groaned and grabbed my ribcage. "We're almost there," I said. "What have you been working on, Richard?"

"I've been trying to organize the *King's Men* and complete our preparations for our performance. But I also investigated the ghost sightings in Gallery Hall."

"Discover anything interesting?" I asked as we reached the doctor's door.

"Perhaps," said Richard, reaching into his pocket. "I found this." He pulled out a handkerchief and handed it to me. It contained white powder.

"What's this?"

"I don't know," said Richard, "but I found the powder on the sill of the doorway where the ghost was seen. I put it in my handkerchief in case it was a clue."

"May I keep it?" I asked as I knocked on the doctor's door.

"Of course," said Richard. "I'll wait for you out here."

The door opened and Doctor Butler smiled at me. "I thought I'd see you today. Please, come in."

"Thank you," I said, as I entered the physician's room. "I took a rather nasty beating yesterday, and my ribs are very painful today."

Edward Wilkinson sat on the examination table. His pant leg was rolled up high on his thigh, revealing the stump where he had lost his leg during the war.

"We meet again," said Edward as he smiled.

"It is my pleasure, sir," I said.

"I was just seeing how Edward is adjusting to his new leg," said Doctor Butler.

"New leg?" I asked. "Sir, if this is a joke, it isn't very funny."

The physician laughed. "I'm not joking at all." He turned to Edward. "Show him."

"I made it myself," said Edward, as he handed me the wooden leg. It was made of three pieces of oak connected with hinges, wrapped in leather, with a shoe covering a wooden foot. Brown leather straps secured it in place, and a cotton base cushioned the spot where it mounted against his thigh.

"This is amazing," I said. "Does it work?"

Edward nodded. "It works pretty well, but sometimes the hinges stick."

"Incredible."

"Thank you," said Edward. "And as an old sheriff, I couldn't resist adding something else." He opened a little door on the wooden leg, removed a small wheel-lock pistol, and handed it to me.

Its small size and unique firing mechanism impressed me. He had made the stock of polished dark walnut and attached a shiny brass cap. There was a smooth hickory ramrod along the bottom of the barrel. Doctor Butler examined my ribs as I turned the weapon over in my hands. "It's different from other pistols I've seen," I said, looking at the firing mechanism.

"That's right," he smiled, a look of pride spreading across his face. "It's self-igniting."

"Really?"

"Yes, it uses iron pyrite."

"Is that as hot as flint and steel?"

Edward laughed. "It burns three times hotter, Will."

"Outstanding," I said, handing the pistol back to him.

"Gentlemen," said the physician. "Please put away your toys."

"Of course," said Edward, securing it back inside his wooden leg. "I'm sorry, doctor."

"Your ribs don't seem to be broken," said Butler. "But I would suggest you put a poultice on it. I'm all out of the proper herbs, but Violet Lewis can help you."

"Thank you," I said, and turned to leave.

"William," said the doctor. "Don't delay. Your ribs aren't broken, but you've been badly hurt. You have a lot of swelling, and your condition could degrade quickly if you don't treat it."

"Don't worry, doctor," I said. "Her shop is right on my way."

***

Richard was waiting patiently for me in the hallway. "Now what?" he asked.

"I have to visit the herbalist for a poultice for my ribs," I said. "And then I want to request an audience with Ravynna."

We continued on to see the herbalist and passed a courtier in the hallway. He looked at us nervously and said, "All hail Ravynna the Witch."

"All hail Ravynna the Witch," we echoed back in unison.

Everywhere we went, terror haunted the palace. People were quiet and seemed afraid to say anything other than praise for the self-proclaimed witch queen. Most looked away from me when I glanced at them, but some stared daggers as we passed. When we came to the herbalist's shop, the door was propped open, and the rich scent of dried herbs and medicine wafted out into the hall. Inside, Violet was grinding dried herbs with a stone mortar and pestle.

"Excuse me," I said. "May we come in?"

Violet looked up and smiled. "Yes, of course," she said as she pulled the hair back from her forehead with her fingers.

"Doctor Butler suggested that you might be able to help me treat this injury," I said, raising my shirt to reveal my bruised ribs.

"Yes, I have a poultice that will help lower the swelling," she reached into a drawer and pulled out a white bandage with a strong medicinal scent. She began tying it around my chest, using great skill to avoid causing me more discomfort.

"I'm sorry you are going through all this," she said as she worked.

"These are tough times," I replied, wincing as she creased a knot.

"I can sympathize with how you feel," she said. "Several years ago, my mother was arrested for witchcraft." Violet wrapped another layer of cloth over the pungent poultice.

"And now a witch is in power," said Richard.

"At least for the moment," said Violet as she focused on her work.

Richard shook his head. "Crowds can be so fickle."

"You must forgive me," Violet said, as she pulled her hair back with both hands and tied it with a small tan strip of cloth. "I've been grinding herbs for medicine all day and I must be a sight to look at."

"Nonsense," said Richard. "You look lovely, my dear."

"Thank you, sir," Violet smiled as she curtsied. "You're Richard Burbage. I saw you in *Romeo and Juliet* when I was in London."

"Oh, you did?" he asked. "Did you like it?"

"Oh yes, very much," she nodded. "As an herbalist, I especially liked the sleeping medicine Juliet used to fake her own death."

"I'm glad you enjoyed it," I said.

"Tell me," said Violet. "What was the potion based on?"

"I'm afraid I'm not an herbalist," I said. "I just wanted a good plot twist. Once I was told of a similar concoction being used in real life, so I worked it into my play. What do you think it could be?"

Violet looked thoughtful. "My guess would be belladonna. It has real medical uses, but it requires skill to mix properly. A single berry could kill a child, but if it was ground, thinned, and weakened, it could cause a catatonic sleep. Not unlike death in appearance." Violet checked the tightness of the bandage. "You could also refine it and make it into a white powder. You could then mix the powder with a liquid and a drop or two would be fatal."

"Or perhaps dust the rim of a chalice," I said. I pictured the killer lightly dusting the shiny cup with white powder and then setting it back in the sacristy to be used for the service. I also imagined him pouring a few drops of belladonna into the wine cruet. Either way would be effective, easy, and untraceable.

"Will," said Richard, snapping me out of my thoughts. "Give her the white powder I found in Gallery Hall."

I handed her the handkerchief. She unfolded it, smelled the powder, and sneezed. "Excuse me!" she said.

"Is it belladonna?" Richard asked.

Violet laughed. "No," she said, and smiled. "It's ordinary flour."

Richard looked embarrassed and glanced at me. "Maybe she would have an educated guess on what killed the priest."

"What priest?" she asked.

I told her the story of the deadly Communion service, and the suggestion that hebenon was used to poison the priest. Violet's face became pale. She looked like she was going to be sick, and pressed her hand to her mouth. I realized my description of the appearance of the murdered priest was a bit too graphic.

"I'm sorry," I said. "I'm afraid I've become too comfortable with these gruesome matters."

"I'm sorry, too," said Violet, regaining her composure. She took a deep breath. "What was your question?"

"What is hebenon?"

"I'm not familiar with it," she said, shrugging her shoulders. "Maybe it's the medical name for the flower henbane."

"Is henbane poisonous?" asked Richard.

"In high-enough concentration it would be lethal."

"Smell this," I said, handing her the bottle I had found in the room under the palace. She took a whiff and turned her head away. "It's belladonna." She wrinkled her nose.

Richard looked at me. "Juliet's sleeping potion."

"Or perhaps the poison that killed King Hamlet," I said, carefully lowering my shirt over the poultice. "Or maybe a priest."

***

We left Violet's place and continued on our way. We passed Thomas and Robert Winter who were talking with a group of men. They were deeply involved in a serious discussion and spoke in hushed voices. They didn't seem to notice us as we walked past.

Once we were well out of sight, I turned to Richard. "Could you please do me a favor?"

"Of course."

"Try to use your charming personality to befriend the Winter brothers. Maybe you can learn what they are up to."

Richard shrugged. "Why do you think they are up to anything?"

"I don't know," I said. "But I think there's more going on with them than meets the eye."

Richard smiled. "I'll check into it."

"Thank you," I said. Up ahead was the door to Ravynna's room. Two guards were posted outside. "I'm going to try to speak with Anne. Find me later."

Richard nodded his head and started walking back the way we came. I straightened my clothes, ran my fingers through my hair, and walked up to the two guards.

"Her Majesty has been asking to see you," said a guard as he knocked on the witch's door.

From inside, her powerful voice said, "Who dares disturb Ravynna the Witch?"

Terror surged through me. The guard glanced at me with fear in his eyes.

"Begging your pardon, my lady," said the guard, and cleared his throat. "But William Shakespeare is here to see you."

"Send him in," replied the wicked voice. "And don't disturb me again!"

"Yes, my lady," said the guard, opening the door for me. "And just to be clear, it was *Barnard* who disturbed you, my queen. Not Avery."

As I entered the witch's room, the other guard whispered sarcastically, "Thanks a lot, Avery."

The room was bright with natural light streaming through the many glass windows. In front of me was a grand dining table covered with rich foods.

Ravynna stood at the head of the table. She looked at me haughtily and commanded, "Bow before your queen!"

Shocked, I bowed low.

Her rich laughter filled the room. "Well," she said. "I guess you're not the only actor in the family!"

Anne ran around the table and hugged me. "Oh Will, I'm so glad you're here! Is Judith all right?"

"Yes, my dear," I said, my eyes filling with tears of joy. "She's all right. How are you?"

"I'm splendid!" she beamed. "I never dreamed I'd be the queen of England!"

"Don't forget about Lady Jane Grey," I said. "The nine days queen."

"I know," said Anne. "Nine days and then beheaded."

"Along with her husband," I added.

"Will, what should we do now? Last night I was in a race against time to save you and Judith. I hurried into costume and makeup, and created the character of Ravynna on the spot. I did improvisation like your actors do at the Globe Theater for practice. But I can't keep this up."

"It was a brilliant move, my dear," I said. "And you're right. You can't keep it up for long. The initial shock and fear from last night will begin to fade among the people. Fury will soon take its place."

Anne began to cry. She threw her arms around me and pressed her head against my chest as she sobbed. I held her in my arms and let her emotions pour out. After a few moments, she pulled back and wiped her eyes.

"Well," she said bravely. "Enough of that. We need to come up with a plan. The first thing we need to do is find the murderer and appease the king."

"I agree," I said. "That's what concerns him the most."

"I suspect Malachi Hunter," said Anne. "The way he turned his allegiance to Ravynna so fast doesn't speak well of his integrity."

"That gives me an idea," I said. "What if we use your power to trick him into revealing all he knows?"

"No," said Anne, shaking her head. "I can't leave this room. I'm afraid people will know I'm pretending right away. When they discover the truth, they'll kill us all."

"Then we'll bring him in here to you," I said. "We will get our set designers to make an area in here that will create a magical ambiance. Our makeup artists and costume designers will help you look the part. Malachi's imagination and fear will do the rest."

"That's a good idea," said Anne. "But what if Malachi isn't the killer? We'll have wasted our opportunity, and it may be our last."

"You're right," I said, scratching my beard. "And I'm also suspicious of a few others."

"Then make a list of suspects and invite them all," said Anne. "This may be our best chance to make the killer show his hand."

"Good idea," I said, smiling at my wife.

Anne walked to the window and gazed outside for a moment. She then turned back to me and smiled. "With a little luck, it just might work."

CHAPTER SIXTEEN

After that, things happened fast. Within an hour, we had the stagehands from our theater company assembled in Anne's room. Together we worked to transform the chamber into a theatrical set fitting for Ravynna the Witch. During my years at the Globe Theatre, I learned that with the right environment, people will believe almost anything. And in the words of Alban, *As you believe, so is it.* So, our set designers went to work, and our costume and makeup staff began polishing Anne to look the part.

It relieved our stagehands to learn that Anne was playing a role last night. They said that they had believed she really was Ravynna the Witch. Anne seemed both pleased and disturbed by the ease at which her long-term friends could believe she had secretly been a wicked witch. And she took little comfort when Judith told her that she personally was relatively sure it wasn't true.

The familiar sounds of our stagehands at work calmed me. Finally, I was back in my element. Richard Burbage would play the spokesman for Ravynna, so he could manipulate the crowd and allow Anne to maintain an air of mystery. Anne began rehearsing her routine, and I made a list of the suspects that we would want to question. Thomas and Robert Winter came to mind. *Why were they so mysterious?* I also had my suspicions about the ambitious priest, Jeremiah Talbot. I wanted everyone related to the murder in any way to be there, even if they weren't a suspect. My list was growing. And of course, there was Malachi Hunter. The way Hunter switched his allegiance so quickly was disturbing and needed to be explored.

Malachi had told me about his witch hunting days when he was in Scotland; he seemed frightened by the experience, despite his outward bravado. He told me he was involved in the trial and execution of Janet Wishart. That gave me an idea. What if Ravynna the Witch "summoned" the ghost of Janet Wishart? I was already working on the ghost of Hamlet's father for my new play. Why not adapt the idea for this situation?

As I told Richard and Anne about my little scheme, I felt a smile spread across my face.

"I love it!" said Anne, smiling. "He will be so frightened; he will break and tell us everything."

"I like it too," said Richard. "What did Malachi tell you about it?"

"Well, it happened during the Scottish Witch Panic of 1597. They tried four hundred women and men as witches. Malachi was a witch-pricker. He and the others tortured and sentenced to death more than a hundred people. Janet Wishart and her son were among the executed."

"How was she executed?" asked Anne.

"Death by hanging, then they burned her body."

"So, Anne will pretend to summon Wishart's ghost," said Richard. "An excellent plan, but there's one problem. The actors in the *King's Men* are working with performers from other acting companies. If we pull them to do this instead, it will increase the odds of our secret leaking out. And if we raise suspicions, we might be caught before we solve the mystery."

"And their anger at being fooled could prove deadly," said Anne, the color draining from her face.

"Maybe we could find someone outside the company to play the ghost of the murdered witch," I suggested.

"Yes," Richard said. "But who?"

"Richard," I said. "What do you think of using Violet Lewis?"

He shrugged. "Why her?"

"She loves the theater, so she may have a hidden talent for acting," I said. "Also, we have formed a bond with her. Other than her, I'm not sure who else outside of our company that we could trust. Plus, she sympathizes with our cause."

Richard nodded his head. "I agree."

We sent for Violet to come to Ravynna's chambers, and we continued to work out the details of our performance. It was exciting to be conspiring together as a team once again. I felt hopeful for the first time since this adventure began.

***

When Violet Lewis came into the room, her eyes were wide with terror. Being summoned to the room of Ravynna the Witch had that effect on people.

"Don't worry," I told her. "Everything is all right."

"Sir, please know that I respect the Witch Queen. She has my full support, my full allegiance." Violet looked frightened. "I hope Her Majesty didn't read my thoughts, sir."

I smiled at her. "Nothing like that, my dear."

Violet looked around at the stagehands working. "Sir, if I may ask, what is going on here?"

"That's why we wanted to see you."

"*We*? Who else wants to see me?"

Anne walked up behind her, and Violet turned and gasped when she saw my wife. Violet dropped to her knees before Anne, and cried out, "All hail Ravynna the Witch!"

The stagehands called back in unison, "All hail Ravynna the Witch!" and smiled at each other.

"Please," said Anne, taking Violet's arms and helping her up. "There is no need for that."

"Violet," I said. "Can we trust you?"

"Of course, sir," she replied, looking confused.

"Violet," said Anne. "I'm not really a witch. It was all just an act to save William and the girls. Do you understand?"

Violet broke down in tears and lowered her head. Anne glanced at me with worry in her eyes. We were thinking the same thing: maybe including the young herbalist in our plan was a mistake. When Violet raised her head, she looked relieved and her eyes were shining through tears of joy.

"Oh yes, ma'am," she smiled, wiping away her tears. "Yes, I do, I understand completely."

"Good," said Anne, looking as relieved as I was. "Violet, we need your help. So, I will ask you again. Can we trust you?"

"Oh yes," Violet nodded. "I want to help in any way I can."

"Very good," I said. "Now, here's what we need you to do…"

***

The set for the Witch's Throne Room looked perfect. We darkened the chamber, with lighting only on the raised area where we placed a single royal chair for Ravynna the Witch. Her throne was crafted from dark wood, with exquisite carvings befitting the Witch Queen of England. We placed two glowing charcoal pots on each side of the chair, with burning candles behind them to give the rising smoke an eerie glow. We also put one iron charcoal pot in front of her throne to cast a glowing orange light on her face. Behind her chair, we draped a very thin cloth from the floor to the ceiling to be used as a backdrop. Hidden behind the thin cloth, we placed dry wood and kindling in an iron pot, with a lighted candle placed next to it so we could light the fire at the perfect time. We had used the effect before on stage. The thin cloth with the light behind it would cast mysterious shadows of anything standing between the light and the curtain. If all went according to our plans, it would create a chilling effect.

Looking out at the gathering crowd, I felt a familiar flutter in my stomach. Back stage, Anne looked calm. Violet brought her a drink, and Anne sipped it in a relaxed manner. Despite her outward tranquility, I didn't want to disturb Anne. She was preparing for the most important performance of her life. Besides, I was nervous enough for the both of us. We had invited a select group of people related to the murder. We also asked Myles Lewis to bring a few servants to make King James and his staff comfortable.

"Lord have mercy," I mumbled, as the two nearly deaf servants, Henry and Alyce, entered the room. I would have preferred anyone else. With them were two other servants I hadn't seen before. I looked for Violet's sisters, Elspet and Janet, and I was relieved they weren't there. I trusted Violet, but I was also concerned that sharing this secret with her sisters would be too great of a temptation for her.

96

The king agreed to attend and sat in the back of the room; on each side of him stood a guard. Near the king sat many of the Anglican and Puritan clergy. Archbishop Whitgift was there, along with Richard Bancroft. Oliver Fletcher and a few others sat with them. John Reynolds was nearby, too, and several other Puritan leaders.

Closer to the stage, Thomas and Robert Winter were speaking in hushed voices to each other. Near them were a few courtiers who had been at the chapel on the day of the murder. Also present was William Butler, the king's physician. In the seats in front of them sat Jeremiah Talbot, the assisting priest on the day of the murder. And Lady Sarah Goody and a few of her friends were sitting in the second row.

Edward Wilkinson, the retired sheriff, sat on the front row. He wasn't a suspect, but we had few allies, and I thought he may be helpful if trouble arose. But I kept our real plan a secret from him. For the moment, the fewer who knew the whole truth, the better. I was both nervous and comforted to know that he had a pistol hidden in his wooden leg.

I brushed my hair back, straightened my clothes, and stepped out to mingle with the crowd and build their expectations. Malachi Hunter stood when I entered the room and he walked over to speak with me.

"Thank you for ensuring that I was invited to this most prestigious gathering," said Malachi. "It is a bold new day for England."

"Indeed," I said. "But I have to warn you, Her Majesty is not happy."

"She's not?" Malachi's smile faded. "Well, of course not. Not everyone here is a loyal supporter of hers like I am. She needs to root out any disloyalty." Malachi fixed me with his dreadful stare. "No matter where that disloyalty may lie."

"You'll excuse me," I said, and I turned to speak with others in the room.

Malachi placed his hand on my arm, and I looked back at him. "You will let the Witch Queen know that I am an experienced torturer, won't you? And that I'm ready to serve her in this capacity if needed?"

"Trust me," I smiled. "She already knows."

"Of course," he responded. "Ravynna sees all and knows all."

"Yes," I paused, and then added, "Ravynna even knows your thoughts."

Malachi swallowed hard and nodded.

I continued through the crowd, building their expectation that something magical and supernatural was about to happen. Alban had told me about the power of faith, and so I worked on building their belief. I suggested, I hinted, but I never outright said what they were about to see. The dominant mood in the room was fear. Incense filled the air as Richard Burbage took to the stage.

"Your attention, please. In a few moments, Ravynna the Witch Queen will condescend to address you," said Richard. He looked regal, and his eyes were dark and penetrating. The glowing embers of the charcoal fire in front of the witch's chair cast a ghastly light on his dark countenance. A chill ran through me. "You will not speak unless you are spoken to," he continued. "You will answer immediately and truthfully if you are addressed."

Someone whispered in the front row, and Richard glared at him so long and with such venom that it even made me uncomfortable.

"And if you lie," Richard paused for effect, "Ravynna will know."

I swallowed hard and glanced at the faces around the room. Richard's words and the mysterious environment entranced them.

"Ladies and gentlemen, Ravynna the Witch!"

Richard threw a pinch of flash powder into the glowing iron pot in front of him, which flashed with a small, sudden explosion. The crowd gasped as the light and fire flared up, and the scent of sulfur flooded the room. For a moment, we were all blinded by the light. When the smoke cleared and our eyes adjusted, Richard was gone and there sat upon the throne a mysterious figure who seemed to appear out of thin air.

"All hail Ravynna the Witch!" I said in a loud and majestic voice.

And the crowd echoed together, "All hail Ravynna the Witch!"

CHAPTER SEVENTEEN

The dark room was cold, and the incense was thick. Ravynna the Witch sat on her royal throne, her face drenched in the glowing orange light of the burning embers. Even though I knew the truth, I felt terror rising in my chest. I almost believed that Anne truly was Ravynna the Witch, and I was afraid. The crowd whispered to each other.

"Silence!" thundered the voice of the witch. The room became quiet, and Anne let the tension rise and then hang in the air. After what seemed like an eternity, she spoke.

"Why do you try the patience of your queen? Why do you weary me by having to discipline you like children? Why must I prove my power before you will listen?"

Ravynna raised her right hand slowly. As she did, a lute we placed on the floor to her right rose into the air. The crowd gasped as the lute rose higher until it was about seven feet in the air. When Ravynna stopped raising her right hand, the lute stopped rising and hung in the cold air. Then Ravynna began strumming her fingers, and as she did so, lute music filled the chamber. Even though she was ten feet away from the levitating lute, the haunting melody filled the room.

Everything was working perfectly. Unbeknownst to the audience, stagehands pulled thin strings from behind the scenes, making the lute rise on a pulley. And hidden behind the curtain was a lute player, strumming a melancholy tune. I glanced around at the faces in the crowd; they were transfixed.

Ravynna then raised her left hand, and a flute that we had placed to her left rose into the air. When it reached the same height as the lute, she began fluttering her fingers on her left hand. The flute played, filling the air with eerie music. And all the while, our stagehands were making the real magic and the real music from behind the scenes.

Ravynna dropped her hands, and the music stopped as the two instruments crashed to the floor. She took a small wax doll and held it up for the audience to see. She tied strings to it and displayed it as a marionette.

"You," she said, pointing at me. "Arise."

"I will not," I said.

Ravynna cackled a cruel laugh. She pulled the strings, making the wax marionette stand up. I stood up, as if pulled by invisible strings. She made the doll dance, and I matched the dance exactly, just like we had practiced. She then dropped the strings, and I fell to the floor like a rag doll, dropped by a child who had grown tired of playing with it. I crawled back to my seat. The crowd gasped and began whispering to each other.

"Silence!" Ravynna again addressed the crowd.

"I am not an entertainer, here for your amusement," she said. "Nor am I a fortune teller, begging for a few coins to reveal your pathetic future. I am Ravynna the Witch, and the veil between the worlds is thin to me. I have done this demonstration for your benefit, so you will know my power and my grace."

I looked around the room, and everyone looked terrified. I wanted to glance behind me to see the king's face, but I feared it would break the spell the crowd was under.

"There has been blood spilled in this palace," Ravynna continued. "And this blood has been taken without my permission. And what is worse, this blood has not been dedicated to my glory. Martin Page, the royal priest, has been murdered while saying Mass in the Royal Chapel. I have no qualms with his murder, except that it was done without my consent. Furthermore, it was done in a bungled attempt to murder the king. And as the High Queen of England, I cannot let this deed pass unpunished."

"Take heed, you who sit in the Queen's Chambers," Richard Burbage said as he entered from behind the audience. He surprised the crowd with his loud voice. "You are here by the order of the Witch Queen, and you will do as you are told. I warn you, Ravynna will find the one who dared spill human blood without her permission. The Witch Queen is not without mercy. But if you make her drag the truth out of you, the punishment for all will be unbearable."

The crowd was silent. A man made the sign of the cross, and a woman by his side began crying. We had them right where we wanted them. It was time for the questioning to begin.

"You!" Ravynna pointed at Thomas Winter. "Stand and face your queen."

Thomas sat and stared at Ravynna. His eyes were defiant. *Oh no*, I thought. *She started with Thomas, and he will resist.*

"Stand!" she commanded. If Anne was afraid, she wasn't showing it.

Thomas stood, but still looked defiant.

"Yes," he said, never blinking. "What does the lady require?" Thomas paused a moment, and then added with a hint of sarcasm, "My queen."

"I require the truth," said Ravynna. "Why are you here at Hampton Court Palace?"

"My business is my own," said Thomas Winter.

"Your business, and the business of everyone in England, exists solely at the pleasure of Ravynna the Witch," said Richard.

"Whatever you say," responded Thomas, and sat down.

"How dare you sit when being addressed by your queen?" thundered Ravynna. "I shall strike you dead!"

"Please, Your Majesty," said Robert Winter, standing. "My brother is not well. I ask your forgiveness for his insolence."

"And you shall have it," said Ravynna. "But only if you answer in his proxy."

"I will be happy to," said Robert Winter. "Our business here is intellectual, nothing more."

"Intellectual?" asked Ravynna. "What do you mean?"

"We are on a fact-finding mission, Your Majesty, and that is all."

"Are you Puritans?" she asked. "Or Anglicans? Do not lie. Ravynna has her ways of finding the truth."

"We are neither, Your Majesty," said Robert. "We represent an overlooked faction in this debate."

"And what faction is that?" asked King James from the back of the room.

Thomas Winter stood and faced the king. "We are proud to be faithful Roman Catholics, Your Majesty."

"Roman Catholics have enjoyed tolerance in England since the Elizabethan Settlement," said Robert Winter.

"That initial tolerance waned, however," added Thomas, "in the later years of Queen Elizabeth's reign."

"You need not labor this point," said King James. "I was baptized Roman Catholic, but raised Presbyterian." The king glanced at the Puritans, who seemed pleased that he was raised protestant. And then he added, "At the moment, however, I'm leaning Anglican."

"Enough," said Ravynna. "I have no dog in your petty religious fight. Sit down, both of you."

The Winter brothers glanced at each other and then sat.

Well, I thought. *That explains why they are at Hampton Court and why they are so serious and secretive.* The religious tensions in England were high, and a tiny spark could set the country ablaze.

"Arise," Ravynna pointed at Father Jeremiah Talbot. "Stand before your queen."

Father Talbot stood and faced the witch, his hands clasped behind his back.

"You are ambitious," said Ravynna. "And you crave advancement in your career."

"Only if it will allow me to better serve my Lord and my king," said Talbot. And then he added, "Or my queen, should that be the case."

"I applaud ambition, and the use of murder to gain a higher rank appeals to my sensibilities," said Ravynna with a wicked smile. "But only in the service of my agenda. Regicide is troubling to me, now that I have rightfully ascended to my throne."

"If you are asking if I would kill King James, I most certainly would not," said Father Talbot. "I believe strongly in the divine right of kings."

"What do you mean?"

"The king rules by God's authority, and by God's authority alone," said Talbot. "And so, only divine authority can depose a monarch. Man cannot do it," the young priest paused. "Nor can a witch."

"How dare you!" thundered Richard Burbage, playing his role as a loyal subject of the Witch Queen to the hilt.

"Stop," Ravynna raised her hand. "We shall let this slight pass. At least for now. You may be seated."

Father Talbot sat, and a fellow priest next to him patted him on the back. I was afraid. A few brave souls were challenging the witch. This would embolden others to doubt her powers, and we still needed to gain more information. It was time for the witch to summon the ghost of Janet Wishart.

"The time has come to bring a witness from the other side," said Ravynna. "The veil between the worlds is thin for Ravynna. I can part the curtains at will and summon spirits to do my bidding. I demand complete silence. I shall go into a trance and you must not disturb me."

Richard Burbage came forward with a sack filled with ground salt. He began sprinkling it in a circle around Ravynna. When he had completed the circle, he put a handful of dried lavender in each of the three burning pots. Ravynna took a deep breath and summoned the ghost of the witch.

"It is I, the Witch of Eden. It is I, the Witch of Endor. I call to the other world for one of the spirits in prison."

I glanced around at the crowd. The people were wrapped in awe. Anne was gaining them back, and terror filled their eyes.

"I call for Janet Wishart, the witch of Aberdeen."

Malachi let out a gasp, his eyes transfixed on the stage.

Ravynna lowered her head and became silent. The incense in the air was very thick now, and it was getting harder to breathe. Smoke filled the air. The glowing light from the coals in the cauldrons created a terrifying atmosphere. Ravynna threw back her head and let out her breath. She shook from head to toe, dropped her head, and became still.

After a moment, there was a *thump* followed by something scraping against the floor to Anne's right. The sound continued and was rhythmic and hypnotic. *Thump, scrape, thump, scrape, thump, scrape.* Out of the darkness stepped the figure of a woman dressed in a long white shroud with a veil. She would take one step, and then drag her other leg behind her. The ghostly figure held her head stiff, and to one side.

Nice touch, Violet. I thought. *Janet Wishart was hanged, so her neck must have been broken.*

She turned to the crowd and cried out in a raspy voice: "Who dares disturb the ghost of Janet Wishart?"

Very good! I thought. *She is a great actor.*

Even I almost believed that this truly was the ghost of the witch of Aberdeen. At that moment, I felt cold fingers touch my arm. It startled me, sending an icy shiver up my spine. I glanced over, and I couldn't believe my eyes.

It was Violet Lewis.

CHAPTER EIGHTEEN

Violet's eyes were intense, and she looked like she had been crying. Whatever had happened would have to wait. The ghost of Janet Wishart was facing the crowd. She was clad in a white-lace dress, and the veil covering her face hid her features. I could barely see her nose and mouth, but the veil completely hid her eyes. The glowing orange and red light from the dying embers flickered on her form, framing her in shadows and rising smoke. It filled me with terror. The smell of the incense was so thick and sweet that I thought I would be sick. There was something familiar within the smoke of the burning incense. My mind searched to identify what it was. And then I remembered. It was the same scent as the liquid in the vial I found. My stomach churned as I took out a handkerchief and covered my nose.

"My spirit has returned, hungry for vengeance," said the ghost. "My powers have grown since crossing to the other side. I sense in this room someone who was at my trial for witchcraft."

The ghost scanned the crowd, searching back and forth among the darkened faces. She crept closer to the crowd; her neck hung stiffly to one side. Walking across the stage, she dragged her broken leg behind her. *Thump, scrape, thump, scrape, thump, scrape.* A woman on the second row covered her ears to block out the horrifying sound; a man put his arm around his wife to comfort her.

The ghost started on the left side of the crowd and walked down the row—*Thump, scrape, thump, scrape, thump, scrape*—looking into the face of each person. When she came to a certain man, she stopped and turned towards him. She pointed a long bony finger at him. It was Malachi Hunter.

"You!" she screeched. "I recognize your face. Where do I know you from?"

Malachi said nothing. He locked his eyes on the ghost of the witch. Fear paralyzed him.

"Answer me!" thundered the ghost.

Malachi was trying to speak, but terror made him mute. After a moment, he pulled his eyes away from the ghost and squeezed them tight. Then he spoke.

"Begging your pardon, ma'am," he whispered. "I am—"

"Speak up!" said the ghost.

"I am Malachi Hunter," he blurted. "And I don't think I've had the pleasure—"

"Oh yes," said the ghost. "Now I remember you."

"I'm flattered," said Malachi, keeping his eyes shut in terror.

"Flattered, are you? Then you will be happy to know that I remember even more about you."

"Thank you, ma'am," he said, opening his eyes. "But I don't want to monopolize your time—"

"Time?" said the witch. "I have nothing but time. Time to remember. Time to think. Time to play the sham of my trial over and over in my mind. Time to remember the face of my torturer." The witch paused. "Time to remember your face, Malachi Hunter."

Malachi was shaken to his core. His hands were trembling, and he kept his eyes on the floor in front of him.

"I'm sorry, ma'am," said Malachi. "I'm so sorry."

"I remember the days of questioning," said the ghost. "No food, no water. I remember cruel tests."

"I am so sorry, ma'am," mumbled Malachi.

"There was the swimming test," said the ghost. "When you and a few others dragged me to a filthy pond, bound my hands, and pushed me in to see if the water would reject my body. I was examined from head to toe for the Devil's mark on my skin, with crowds of people watching. And then there was the worst test of all."

"And what test was that, ma'am?" asked Malachi.

"Perhaps you would like to guess," said the ghost.

Malachi Hunter was silent. The room continued to fill with thick incense. The glowing coals flickered and the smoke continued to rise.

"I… I'm afraid…" Malachi cleared his throat. "I'm afraid I don't know, ma'am."

"You don't know?"

"No, ma'am."

"You?" she said. "A highly trained, professional witch-pricker. You of all people don't know the worst torture?"

Malachi was silent.

"Stand up," said the ghost.

Malachi remained glued to his seat.

"Stand up!" thundered the ghost.

Malachi stood up, but kept his eyes focused on the floor.

The witch's ghost turned and said to the crowd, "The most terrible torture of all was the witch pricking."

She moved across the front row, speaking to the crowd as she walked. "Who here knows what witch pricking is?" *Thump, scrape, thump, scrape, thump, scrape.*

The crowd was silent.

"Come now," said the ghost in her raspy voice. "We are all friends here. Surely someone knows what witch pricking is."

Again, no response.

"Well then," said the ghost, pointing at Malachi. "Why don't you share with everyone your wealth of knowledge on witch pricking? You, like the other professional witch-prickers, have had a massive amount of expert training on this matter. I believe some of you may have even read a tiny booklet on it. Surely with that level of higher education you can tell these simple people about your noble profession."

Malachi looked up. "Witches have the Devil's mark, which keeps them from experiencing pain. Piercing them with pins is the only way of determining if they have the mark."

"Yes," said the ghost. "So they say. And witch-prickers numb the suspected witches first, is that not so?"

"Yes, ma'am," said Malachi. "Some do."

"And you yourself have done this?"

Malachi was silent.

"Answer me!"

"Yes, my lady."

"Now why would you do a thing like that? Could it be because anyone would feel excruciating pain after being poked by a sharp needle? Could it be that the only way to make someone appear not to sense pain would be to numb them first?"

"It was only because I was trying to weed out the false witches," said Malachi. "I am a loyal supporter of Ravynna, the Witch Queen. I only wanted to expose the fakers, that's all. Never real witches."

I glanced at my wife. She was still sitting slumped over in her chair. My heart jumped into my throat. *What if Anne wasn't acting?*

"Bah!" said the ghost. "Ravynna is nothing but a fraud. She fools the weak-minded with parlor tricks. She performs a role, and you applaud. She plays a tune, and you dance. Here stands before you a real witch, and you are too stupid to realize it. If anyone is to be crowned the Witch Queen of England, it should be me, not her. Bow before me!"

Malachi dropped to his knees before the ghost.

"So," said the ghost. "You are loyal to Ravynna, are you?"

"No, ma'am."

"No?" she asked. "But you just said that you were her loyal subject."

"No ma'am," said Malachi. "I was only testing her, ma'am. To find out if she is a real witch."

"And is she a real witch?"

"No ma'am," said Malachi.

"Then what is she?"

"She is a fraud."

The crowd gasped. Malachi glanced up, but then lowered his eyes again.

"And to whom are you loyal?"

"To you, my lady."

"Louder please."

"To you, my lady."

"Shout it," said the ghost.

"To you, my lady!" said Malachi, and then he burst into tears.

"Stay on your knees, you coward."

The ghost turned and walked up and down the front of the crowd. *Thump, scrape, thump, scrape, thump, scrape.* When she passed in front of me, I mustered every drop of courage I had and looked into the face of the ghost. I still could only make out a general shape behind her white veil. The witch then stopped and turned to address the crowd.

"Is there no innocence here?" she asked. "Is there no virtue?"

The crowd was silent. The ghost continued.

"You are all guilty, for you have all had a part in this tragedy. Your part may have been small or great, but you all have blood on your hands. You who have stood by in silence as they burned your friends and family at the stake. You who have supported a king who has made it his mission to persecute witches. Yes, all of you are guilty," she paused. "But some are more guilty than others."

The witch resumed her silent march. *Thump, scrape, thump, scrape, thump, scrape.* When she came to the end of the row, she turned and made her way back, step by step. *Thump, scrape, thump, scrape, thump, scrape.* This time when she passed by me, I noticed that the sweet scent from the glass vial was strong. When she reached the center of the room, she stopped and again addressed the crowd.

"You here who are loyal to King James, stand up."

There was a long silence. Someone in the crowd was crying.

"Is no one loyal to King James?"

The silence became unbearable. I took a deep breath and stood up.

"Well, well, well," said the ghost. "The king's Witchfinder General is his only loyal servant."

"I am sure there are others," I said, hoping I sounded braver than I felt.

"I wouldn't be so sure," said the ghost. "I can understand now why someone tried to murder the king. He has inspired so little devotion."

The ghost began walking towards me. *Thump, scrape, thump, scrape, thump, scrape.* It seemed to take an eternity for her to reach me. When she did, she spoke to me, but she meant it for everyone to hear.

"I pity you, Witchfinder General. With so many disloyal subjects, finding the killer will be impossible."

"I hope it is not as desperate as you suggest," I answered.

"Ha!" said the ghost.

And then someone stood. It was William Butler, the court physician. He looked defiant and faced the witch.

"So," said the ghost. "There is one other. And this one is known for his courage coming from a bottle." She turned to me. "Can you solve a murder with a staff of one?"

And then something wonderful happened. Archbishop Whitgift stood, followed by Richard Bancroft, Jeremiah Talbot, and John Reynolds. The rest of the Anglicans and Puritans all stood together as one, facing the ghost. They seemed to be a brotherhood for the first time since all this began. I smiled despite the gravity of the situation.

"I'm surprised," said the ghost. "Even rats are smart enough to leave a ship when it is sinking."

For the first time, she sounded unsure of herself. I gazed around the room as others stood. Oliver Fletcher, Edward Wilkinson, and the king's staff were all standing. Most of the room was standing now. I glanced back at King James and he looked pleased.

"Witchfinder General," said the ghost. "It appears your list of suspects is growing shorter. Perhaps there may be hope for you after all. And perhaps I can help you by reducing your list of suspects even more."

The crowd was silent as she began her walk. *Thump, scrape, thump, scrape, thump, scrape.* The incense was thick. I had to have fresh air soon. The room that had been so cold at the start of this gathering was now stifling hot. I was afraid I would pass out. The coals were dying down, and she continued to walk. *Thump, scrape, thump, scrape, thump, scrape.*

The ghost then stopped in front of Malachi Hunter, who was still kneeling on the floor.

"Look at me," said the ghost.

Malachi kept his eyes lowered.

"Look at me!" the ghost commanded.

Malachi looked up at the ghost. She stared at him for a moment. And then the blade of a knife shone in her hand, reflecting the dying light. Like a flash of lightening, she slashed her knife across his throat. Malachi grabbed his throat as blood poured through his hands and down his chest. The ghost backed away into the darkness, blood splattering on her white dress. William Butler ran forward. Malachi Hunter dropped to the floor. The crowd swirled around his body, and I pushed my way through the throng. But there was nothing any of us could do to help him.

Malachi Hunter was dead.

CHAPTER NINETEEN

The chamber erupted in shouts and cries. Guards rushed King James from the room. A woman cradled Malachi in her arms and wept. She looked up at me, tears streaming from her eyes. "He wasn't a bad man," she said. "He was just very afraid." I realized then that she was his wife, and tears ran down my cheeks.

"I am so sorry this happened," I said. "I'm sorry you had to witness this."

Malachi's wife turned her head and stroked his hair. Her tears fell like drops of rain on the face of her beloved. Her tenderness moved me deeply. I wiped the tears from my eyes.

Thoughts of my wife filled my mind, and I rushed to check on Anne. Still sitting slumped in her chair, Anne's head hung down and she was nonresponsive. I opened her left eyelid; only the white was showing.

"Doctor Butler!" I called. "Doctor Butler, come quick!"

William Butler pushed his way through the crowd surrounding Malachi's body and came to my side. He checked her eyes, and then lowered his ear to her mouth to listen for breathing.

"Quiet!" he said to the crowd, but the noise continued. "I said quiet!"

The crowd ignored the doctor's plea as they shouted at each other and ran throughout the room. Doctor Butler looked at me. "Get me a mirror."

I ran to Anne's vanity, grabbed her mirror, and brought it back to the physician. He held it up to her nose, and the glass steamed.

"Thank the Lord," I said, crossing myself. "She's alive."

"Yes," said Butler. "But just barely. She needs fresh air."

I picked Anne up in my arms. The light of the hallway shown through the open door. I had to get her out fast, but it was a madhouse. The guards were trying to control the crowd and usher people out of the room. In the pandemonium, someone tripped over a pot of coals, and fire erupted. A wall of fire trapped Anne and me, preventing us from escaping. Doctor Butler and most of the others were on the opposite side of the flames, scrambling to get through the door. The crowd was running wild, screaming and trying to escape the burning room. They rushed the door, trampling each other.

"Help us!" I called, but to no avail.

The roaring flames cut us off from the exit. Even if we could fight our way through the blazes, the door was packed with people trying to push through to safety. Smoke, fire, and screams filled the room. I glanced around for another exit, but could find none. There was a sharp tug on my shirt. I turned and looked. It was Violet Lewis.

"This way!" she said as she pulled on my arm.

The carpets were burning as she pulled us through the fire. She led us to a corner of the room where the walls were burning. I glanced back, but the smoke was so heavy that I couldn't see. I couldn't stop coughing violently.

"Through there!" said Violet, and she pointed to the burning wall.

"There's no door!"

"It's a secret panel," said Violet.

She reached her hands into the flames and searched for the release for the hidden door.

"Stop!" I screamed, but she continued. "Violet, stop! Stop!"

Bravely working through the pain, she found the hidden door release she had been looking for, pulled it, and the secret panel opened.

Still holding Anne in my arms, I sprang into the secret passage. I looked back at Violet. Flames danced around her as she dug something out of a pocket in her dress.

"Here, take this," she said, and handed me a folded piece of paper.

"Come on!" I said. "Hurry!"

"I'm not going," she said. "Tell them I am so sorry."

The fire outlined her face as she closed the panel behind us. "No!" I screamed, but to no avail. There was no time to lose; I had to save Anne.

I carried her into the hidden passageway. We continued down the passage as the sound of the fire faded behind us. The tunnel was dark, but the smoke was gone and the air was breathable. I laid Anne on the floor and stuffed the paper Violet had given me into my pocket.

"Anne? Can you hear me?"

Anne began coughing, and she sat up.

"Where am I?" she asked.

I told her what had happened and where we were. I was about to ask her why she passed out during the show, but I sensed someone behind me. I turned to look, but it was too dark to see anything.

"Who's there?"

"Will, is that you?" came a man's voice.

"Yes, I'm William Shakespeare, who are you?"

"It's me," he said. "Edward Wilkinson."

"Thank the Lord," I said, relieved. I was glad to have the former sheriff and adventurer with us.

"Are you all right?" he asked.

"Yes, now we are." I told him about Anne. She was breathing better now and seemed alert.

"Very good," said Edward. "My lady, can you stand?"

"I think so," said Anne. "Give me a hand?"

Bracing her arm, I helped her up. All things considered, she seemed to be all right.

"How did you find us?" Anne asked.

"I'm afraid I wasn't looking for you," said Edward. "I was only trying to escape the fire and save my own skin. I thought the fire would be my last adventure. But then I remembered hearing about a door to a secret passage in the room. I started knocking until I found it."

"I'm glad you did," I said.

"Can you help us get out of here?" Anne asked.

"Yes, I've been fascinated by these tunnels since I first learned about them," said Edward. "I'm hoping the fire is out by now. People were throwing buckets of water on it right before I escaped. But it wouldn't be wise to go back, just in case. Keep going forward. We'll use our fingers to find our way along the wall through the dark. But be careful. There are a lot of passageways through here, and it's easy to get twisted around."

We started walking forward, carefully, one step at a time. Anne and I were going side by side, with Edward walking behind us. It surprised me how well Edward kept up with us. He was skilled at using the new leg he had made. The leg's combination of wood for structure, leather for flexibility, and hinge for movement worked well together. And the wheel-lock pistol hidden inside was a nice touch.

"May I ask a question?" asked Edward.

"Of course," I said.

"The question is for your wife, if that's all right, sir."

"Yes?" said Anne.

"How often does your identity shift between Anne Hathaway and Ravynna the Witch? Does her spirit possess you?" Edward paused, and then added, "No offense, madam, but I don't want to be stuck in this darkness with a witch right now."

"None taken," said Anne.

"Edward," I said. "Ravynna was a role that Anne had to play to buy time. We used it to find answers to questions that we couldn't otherwise. It was the only way of proceeding with the investigation, considering the circumstances."

"I'm sorry we had to deceive you," said Anne.

"So, just to be clear," said Edward. "You were never really a witch?"

"Thankfully, no," said Anne.

"So, Ravynna was your own creation? She's not an actual witch?"

"I hope that doesn't disappoint you," I said, smiling.

"Oh, no indeed," said Edward. "No indeed."

"There's a turn on my right," said Anne.

"And on my left," I said, touching the wall.

"Go to the left," said Edward.

We turned to the left and continued to grope our way along the wall.

"Does the king know your subterfuge about Ravynna?"

"No," I said. "But as soon as we are out of here, we are going to tell everyone the truth."

"Be careful," said Edward. "Crowds can shift allegiance at a moment's notice."

"I know," I said. "But we will take that risk."

"So, there really was a ghost?" asked Anne.

"Yes," I said, putting my hand on her shoulder. "It was terrifying."

"By the way," said Edward, "do you know what happened to the ghost? I was watching Malachi, and I didn't see where she went."

"After she killed Malachi, she backed away and vanished."

"Vanished?" he asked. "You saw her vanish?"

"Yes," I said, and then I thought for a moment. "Actually, I guess not, now that you mention it."

"Exactly what did you see?" asked Edward.

I inched forward with my toes and felt a drop off.

"Anne, stop," I said. "I can't feel the floor with my toes. It must be a drop off."

"It's okay," said Edward. "It's a stairway leading down. It's the right way to go if we want to get out of here."

"I'm glad we have a guide who knows the way," said Anne.

Carefully, I put my foot over the edge. Not having anything to hold on to made me nervous. I searched around with my toes and was delighted to feel the first step.

"It's okay," I said. "I found the first step."

"You are in a spiral staircase," said Edward. "Feel around until you find a handrail."

I reached out in front of me and felt the cold metal of a handrail. "Got it." I helped Anne onto the first step. We descended. Edward was behind us, his wooden leg clicking on each step. My thoughts drifted back to being under the palace the day before, and the eerie chanting. I wondered about the sound of whatever it was that had pursued me. I was happy to have a retired sheriff with us. And it brought me comfort to know that he had his pistol, and years of experience.

"So," said Edward. "What did you see after the ghost killed Malachi Hunter?"

"Can we please not talk about this now?" asked Anne. "I'd rather not think about ghosts of witches murdering people if you don't mind."

"Of course, my dear," I said. "I'm afraid I have nothing to report, anyway. Malachi's blood splattered on the ghost's dress as she backed away. I focused on Malachi after that."

"Hmm," said Edward. "That's strange."

We reached the bottom step.

"What's strange?" asked Anne.

"You said the blood splattered on the ghost's dress."

"That's right," I said, inching my way forward down the passageway. "I don't understand your point."

"Well," he replied. "How could blood stain a ghost's clothes?"

"You're right!" I said.

"That means she wasn't really a ghost," said Anne.

"Probably not," said the old soldier and sheriff. "But anything is possible."

We felt the smooth walls along the passageway for guidance. My thoughts drifted back to being in the palace's underground the day before.

"Look," said Anne.

Up ahead was a glimmer of light. It seemed to be shining down from above.

"Thank heaven," I said, and I called back to Edward. "There's light ahead!"

"Just a moment," said Edward. "The hinge on my leg has locked up again."

Edward stopped to work on his leg. There were sounds of clicks and snaps as he tried to fix the hinge.

"Will," Anne whispered to me. "Do you think we could keep going towards the light? I want out of here as soon as possible."

"Edward," I called. "We are going to move towards the light."

"Very good," said Edward. "Don't worry about me. I have to tinker with my homemade leg all the time. It's just a little more difficult in the dark."

"Can I help you?" I asked.

"No, thank you," he said.

Anne and I started walking towards the light. Edward continued working behind us. We came closer to the light, and I could see stairs.

"Edward," I called. "There are stairs ahead."

"That's what we're looking for," said Edward.

There was a loud pop, and Edward said, "Oh, hang it all, let's get out of here and I'll fix this locked hinge later."

Relieved, I looked at Anne. I could just make out her face now in the pale light streaming from above. I took her arm and started towards the stairway.

And that's when it happened.

There was a long scraping sound, followed by a footstep. The pattern continued, over and over again. Anne and I froze to the spot and clutched each other tight. I then realized it was the same sound that was pursuing me the day before, when I was in these underground passageways. Terror filled me as I understood what, or rather who, was chasing me through the darkness the day before.

"You!" I said. "You were the one who was following me down here yesterday!"

Edward emerged out of the darkness, dragging his leg on the ground behind him. The light from above shown down on him as he pointed his wheel-lock pistol at us.

"That's right," said Edward. "I'm sorry, but I must insist that you come with me."

CHAPTER TWENTY

Edward's wheel-lock pistol glimmered in the dim light.

"Edward," I stammered. "How could you?"

Anne dropped to her knees on the dirt floor, holding her stomach.

"Anne, are you all right?"

"I'm sick," said Anne. "I think I'm going to pass out."

"Oh no," I said. "Anne, can I—"

Fast as lightening, Anne stood up and threw a fistful of dirt into Edward's eyes. He dropped his pistol and recoiled, rubbing his eyes violently.

"Run!" said Anne.

I reached down and searched on the ground for his pistol. It was lying to the right of where he was standing. I grabbed it and ran with Anne towards the stairwell.

"Stop!" shouted Edward, rubbing his eyes.

Not wasting a moment, we climbed the spiral stairs as fast as we could. When we reached the top, we couldn't find an exit. I stuffed the pistol into my jacket and began feeling along the walls for a latch.

"Look!" said Anne.

On the side wall, there was light outlining what seemed to be a small square door. Anne and I pushed on the square with all our might, and it opened. We were pleased to discover it led outside to the courtyard. It was almost night, and daylight was fading fast.

Dozens of people filled the courtyard, along with tents, wagons, and horses. Campfires dotted the courtyard, surrounded by people cooking their evening meal. I noticed a frightening figure staring at us. He was dressed all in black, with a waxy overcoat and square-topped hat. He was wearing a white mask with glass eye openings, and it had a strange long beak-shaped nose. He carried a cane in his hand.

"Who is that?" Anne asked a woman walking past us.

The woman glanced at the menacing figure. "Oh that?" she said. "That's the Plague Doctor, that is. We all pooled our shillings and hired a plague doctor to come with us. Can't be too careful these days, that's what I say."

The Plague Doctor walked towards us. Anne grabbed my arm and pulled me in another direction. We started walking between the tents and wagons, but the dark figure kept following us. We ducked into an empty tent, hoping he didn't see us. We waited in silence for a moment until we felt the danger had passed.

"Why was he following us?" asked Anne.

Before I could answer, the tent door ripped opened and in walked the Plague Doctor. He ran to Anne and grabbed her.

"You take your hands off her!" I yelled. "Let her go!"

He turned, grabbed me, and hugged me tight. He then pulled back and removed his mask.

It was our oldest daughter, Susanna.

***

Susanna poured each of us a hot cup of tea as we sat in her private tent. Her long flaxen hair draped over her shoulders. I was struck by how much she resembled her mother.

"So," said Susanna as she poured herself a cup of tea. "I realized that even though I'm an adult now, it would have been wise to have gone with you."

"You are always welcome with us," said Anne, smiling. "No matter how grown up you are."

Susanna smiled back at her mother. "Anyway, I realized that if I were to survive this wave of the plague, I would have to get out of London. When I found out this group was going to seek asylum at Hampton Court Palace, I wanted to go. It's a wealthy group, and I was aware I couldn't afford to join them. Nor would I be accepted here on my own. But I convinced them to hire an experienced plague doctor to keep them safe."

"You have medical training now?" asked Anne.

"No," Susanna smiled. "But I've learned the art of acting from the best. I created a character, and I researched my role. I learned a lot about the plague. Fascinating. They think it is spread by miasma."

"What's miasma?" I asked.

"Miasma is foul air," said Susanna. "It's from the Greek, meaning 'pollution.'"

"Oh yes," said Anne. "Judith told me about that. She called it 'night air.'"

"Oh, how is Judith?" said Susanna.

"She has had quite a few adventures since you last saw her," said Anne. "In fact, we all have."

"So, you convinced them you were a plague doctor," I said, beaming with pride at the creativity of my daughter.

"Yes," said Susanna. "But it was the costume that really sold them."

"Yes," I said. "It is impressive."

"I wanted to fill them with awe," said Susanna. "And I also wanted to protect myself from the plague."

She stood and walked over to where her costume was hanging.

"The gloves would keep me from touching a sick person," said Susanna. "And I could use the cane for the same purpose. The glass eye openings would keep out the miasma, the bad air. And the curved, bird-like beak is a kind of filter to keep me from breathing the foul and filthy air. I filled it with dried roses and carnations, along with eucalyptus, peppermint, and a thick vinegar sponge."

"Brilliant," I said.

"Thank you, father," said Susanna. "I made two of the costumes, so I can clean one after inspecting someone for the plague. I keep the other one clean and ready, just in case."

"Susanna," I said. "Can I ask you a favor?"

"Of course."

"Could your mother stay here with you tonight?"

"I would love that," she said. "But why?"

"It's a long story, but she will be safer here," I said. "I'm going back into the palace, and your mother will fill you in on all that has happened."

"Good idea," said Anne. She stood and kissed me on my cheek. "Please be careful, Will."

"Don't worry, my dear," I said. "This will all be over soon."

Susanna gave me a hug and squeezed my hand.

"Don't worry, father," she said. "I will take good care of her here."

I started to step out into the snowy night air, and then I turned back.

"One more thing," I said, my breath flowing out in a white cloud. "Can I borrow one of your plague doctor costumes?"

***

It was late, and the palace was nearly empty as I made my way back to my room. Susanna's plague doctor outfit was packed inside a bag, slung over my shoulder. I opened the door to my room and built a fire to ward off the cold. I was so tired and had to sleep. I ate a hard piece of bread and started to go to bed. But then I noticed a bottle of wine sitting on a small table next to my chair. I sat down facing the fire and picked up the bottle. There was a note tied to it. It said, "Thank you for your excellent work today."

Well, I thought, *at least someone appreciates what I'm trying to do.*

There was a corkscrew next to the bottle, along with a quality crystal goblet. I pulled the cork on the bottle and poured a glass of wine. Normally I didn't drink, but the wine's bright red color called to me. It looked like a fine old bottle from King Henry VIII's famous wine cellar. Taking a sip, I relaxed in my chair as I sat before the fireplace. And then I remembered the note that Violet stuffed in my hand when I was carrying Anne from the burning room. I patted my pocket, found the note, and took it out.

It read:

My dearest darling,

I am so sorry it had to end this way. In the morning, I will be hanged and then burned, along with our son, Thomas. Please take our daughters and leave Scotland. Go to England and change your last name, but please keep my namesake. I love you and our children. I look forward to seeing you all again one day in the next life.

Your loving wife,

Janet Wishart

I took a drink of wine. It was too sweet for my taste. I took another sip and looked at the glass in my hand, the fire burning behind it. And then two glasses of red wine were shining in the firelight. Two glasses of sweet red wine. Too sweet. A strange sweetness. I pulled the glass to my nose and sniffed. The sickly sweet scent of the vial I had found in the sacristy rose to meet my nostrils. I lost control of my hand, and it dropped, spilling the red wine. Time slowed and the fire flickered. My stomach cramped and my vision blurred. I realized then that I had made a fatal mistake. Someone had poisoned the wine. My body was shutting down.

I was dying.

My muscles tightened, and I couldn't move. *So*, I thought. *This is how it will end.* I tried to call out, but could not. My vision dimmed. It would only be a matter of minutes before I would shuffle off this mortal coil. What would the next world be like? I didn't know. But I wondered, in that sleep of death, what dreams may come?

I knew I would only have a few more moments until I would pass into the undiscovered country. I wanted to solve the mystery before I died.

I thought of the murder in the chapel. Whoever did it was trying to kill the king. It wasn't Malachi, my prime suspect. His brutal murder put an end to that theory. Could it have been one of the other Puritans? Or one of the bishops? It seemed unlikely. They all hoped for their side to win out. And they all stood showing their support for the king, despite the threatening ghost of the witch. But if not one of them, who? And why?

I thought of the note Violet gave me. It was a condemned wife's last letter to her husband. What could it mean? Poor Violet. I wondered if she survived the fire. Her last words to me were, *Tell them I'm sorry.* Sorry for what? The letter was signed *Janet Wishart*, the witch of Aberdeen. But why would Violet have it? The note had advised Janet's husband and their children to go to England and change their last names, but to be sure to keep her namesake.

And then I remembered something. Violet's sister's name was Janet. *Janet.* Janet Lewis. *Janet Wishart.* I thought back to my conversation with Violet's two sisters in the bakery. Janet joked with her sister Elspet about wanting to be the queen of England one day. And I remembered the words of the ghost of Janet Wishart, *If anyone is crowned Queen of England, it should be me, not her.* I recalled that the ghost had the same sickly sweet smell of the vial from the sacristy. And of the hallway before the murder. And of the physician's room, where they took the murdered priest's body. And of the—pain shot through my stomach—and of the glass of wine I just drank.

So, Janet Lewis must have pretended to be the ghost of her mother to get revenge on Malachi. Her sister Violet must have told her about the plan for her to play the ghost. Janet did what Violet didn't have the constitution to do. They must have drugged Anne to have full control of the situation. And then Violet came and sat with me to give herself an alibi.

My vision became a tunnel. The roaring fire looked like a tiny speck on the distant horizon. My head throbbed, and I felt waves of hot and cold sweep over me. *What was I just thinking about?* Oh yes, the murderer.

Violet Lewis is an herbalist. She knows about medicines—and poisons. She told Richard and me about belladonna and henbane. Sleeping potions if used in small amounts, but deadly if used in larger quantities. And the white powder that Richard found in Gallery Hall, after the ghost sighting in the hallway. It was flour. Ordinary flour.

That's it. Janet and Elspet were bakers. They must have staged the ghost sighting in Gallery Hall as a diversion. The hallway is outside the royal chapel. The "ghost" appeared right before the deadly Communion service. It would have given the killer a chance to poison the chalice. The same sickly sweet scent was in the hallway, and in the vial I found in the sacristy. Whoever poisoned the chalice must have had access to the sacristy.

Oh no, I thought. *Could it be Alban?* He was the sexton; he would have access to the chalice. But he didn't have a motive or the inclination. It seemed unlikely. My intuition said no.

Who else would have had access to the chalice? Jeremiah Talbot. But he pledged his support to the king in front of everyone, even while under duress. And he believes strongly in the divine right of kings. So, if it wasn't the assisting priest or the sexton, it must have been a servant. And not just any servant, but one with a certain amount of freedom. But they would also need access to the poison, knowledge of its use, and a motive.

I was out of time. My eyes closed as the last drop of life slipped out of me.

"That's it," I thought as I breathed my last breath.

"The killer is Myles Lewis."

CHAPTER TWENTY-ONE

My eyes fluttered and then opened. A brilliant light was shining behind the head of an angelic being. I couldn't make out her face, but I thought it might be Mary, the Mother of Jesus. I had died and had gone to heaven. I breathed a sigh of relief. My lungs hurt. *Why is there pain in heaven?* My vision was blurry, but slowly began to focus.

"Doctor Butler," came a familiar voice. "Father's awake."

"Thank you, Judith," said Doctor Butler.

Doctor Butler's here, I thought. *This can't be heaven.* I tried to sit up. My head was pounding; I laid back down again.

"Easy does it," said Doctor Butler. "Lucky for you, Judith found you last night. She ran to my door and pounded on it until I woke up. We ran back here to your room, and you weren't breathing. We had to put a wooden tube in your throat so you could breathe through the swelling."

"What happened?" I asked, my speech slurring.

"Father," said Judith. "Doctor Butler said you were poisoned."

"And it was a botched job," said the doctor. "Whoever did it used the wrong amount. It still was strong enough to kill you, but not strong enough to do it fast. It bought us a little time. We induced vomiting and gave you medicine. It was a long night. We almost lost you."

Judith brought me water to drink. Slowly this time, I sat up and drank the water.

"How do you feel?" asked Judith.

"Not bad for a man who was poisoned," I said, rubbing my throat. "Did you get the medicine from Violet?" I asked the physician.

"William," he said. "Violet is dead. I'm sorry, I know you were fond of her."

"She died in the fire," said Judith. "Her adventure in this life is over, but her adventures in eternal life are just beginning."

We were silent for a moment. I remembered my deductions from last night. I was sure my theory was correct. Myles Lewis murdered the priest and his daughter Janet murdered Malachi. They wanted revenge on King James and Malachi for what happened to Janet Wishart. Violet provided the poison, or at least that was where they got it. Now I needed hard evidence.

"Thank you, doctor," I said, standing up. "I'm feeling much better."

"Then I'll be going," said Butler. "Be sure to stay in, rest, and send for me if you need me."

"Don't worry, doctor," said Judith. "I'll take care of him."

Judith walked Doctor Butler to the door. They exchanged a few stories of the hard night and said goodbye. My stomach was sore and my head throbbed, but there was no time to waste.

"Judith," I said. "I know who the murderers are. Now we need to prove it."

I told Judith everything. We needed evidence, and we needed it fast before they killed anyone else.

"We have a problem. The palace is on edge," said Judith. "You don't have the same authority as you did before the ghost exposed mother as a fake. People are angry and won't cooperate with you. Also, the Lewis family must suspect that you are onto them."

"Why do you say that?"

"Well, first, they are aware both that you are investigating and that they are guilty," said Judith. "They must suspect you are onto them. And second, you said Violet told you she was sorry, and she gave you the note as a way of atoning for her part in the murders. But why would she do that if she didn't think you were close to finding out? She may even have stayed in the fire so she wouldn't be caught and tortured like her mother. After what happened to Janet Wishart, I don't think any of them will allow you to take them alive."

"All true," I said. I thought for a moment, and I had an idea.

The bag with the plague doctor's costume in it was lying by the bed. I pulled the costume out, showed it to Judith, and told her of my plan. Dressed as the plague doctor, I would demand to inspect their room.

Under the pretense of checking for signs of the plague, I would search for evidence. I dressed for my role and started to leave for their room. But then I remembered Edward's pistol. *Edward*, I thought. *How does he fit into this?* With no time to lose, I hid his wheel-lock pistol in my black cloak and left the room.

Crowds of people moved aside as I strode down the hallway. They had never seen anything like my costume before. I came to Myles Lewis' door and rapped it hard with my cane.

"Open up!"

"Who's there?" Myles's voice came from inside.

"The Plague Doctor, here to inspect for signs of the plague."

The door opened and Myles's eyes became wide as he gazed at my costume. "The Plague Doctor?" he asked.

"That's right," I said. "On orders of the king. Now move aside!"

I pushed passed him and searched their small room. After several minutes, I still had found nothing incriminating.

"Do you live here alone?"

"No sir," said Myles. "My daughters live in the connecting room."

There was an inside door near the dresser. "Open it," I ordered.

"They're not in there," said Myles.

"I need to inspect for the plague," I said. "It will only take a moment. Or if you prefer, I could call the palace guards here so I can complete my inspection."

"No need for that," said Myles, as he opened the door.

Three neatly made beds were in the room, along with a small table, two chairs, and a closet. There was a curtain over the closet door which I pushed back with my cane. Something rectangular was on the floor, covered by a blanket. I removed the blanket; there was a wooden chest under it. I opened the wooden chest and smelled the sickly sweet scent of poison. My stomach turned. There was a handkerchief with the name *Janet Lewis* embroidered on it, along with various other personal items. Several glass vials contained liquid, and underneath them was a white garment and veil. It was a white-lace dress, with dried bloodstains. *The ghost's dress.* My heart pounded. I stood and turned to leave the closet. The last thing I saw was Myles Lewis swinging a wooden club at my face.

And then there was only darkness.

***

When I awoke, there was the sound of chanting.

Astarte, Isis, Diana,
Demeter, Hecate, Kali, Inanna.
Astarte, Isis, Diana,
Demeter, Hecate, Kali, Inanna.

When I opened my eyes, the room was spinning. I tried to sit up, but they had bound me to a cold stone table. Lying flat on my back, I pulled against the restraints. My hands and feet were tied down. Someone had removed my plague doctor's costume, and I was now wearing only my trousers. Flickering candlelight filled the room. There were six human shapes dressed in dark woolen robes with hoods hiding their faces. They walked around me in a circle, moving slowly step by step as they chanted.

Astarte, Isis, Diana,
Demeter, Hecate, Kali, Inanna.
Astarte, Isis, Diana,
Demeter, Hecate, Kali, Inanna.

"Halt!" I heard a male voice shout.

A figure walked out of the shadows. He was a man from the waist up, but he had the legs of a goat. On his head were two horns. The figure seemed to melt at first. His features ran together and then flowed back into place. I closed my eyes tight, took a deep breath, and then reopened them. His face looked familiar. He stared at me, a wicked grin on his face. It was Myles Lewis. Again, his face seemed to melt.

"The Witchfinder General is awake," said Myles. "Our ceremony can now proceed."

"Myles, please," I said. "This won't bring back your wife."

"Oh, but it will," said Myles. "A witch is never truly gone. When the conditions are right, we can bring her back."

My head was a little clearer. It was apparent now that Myles was wearing a costume. His goat legs were made of animal skins attached with string, and his horns were part of an elaborate hat. Alban had told me that some magic was a form of theater. *As above, so below.*

"All that it requires is to exchange a life for a life," said Myles. "And the proper rite."

"But you already killed the priest," I said. "You murdered Martin Page."

"That was an accident," said Myles. "I was trying to kill the king."

Myles walked over to a witch.

"But we are not heartless," said Myles. "We acted fast. We retrieved his body from Doctor Butler's examination room. That drunken physician was a bit too hasty in his pronouncement of death." An evil smile spread across Myles' face. "We made amends."

Myles reached over and lowered the hood that was hiding the face of the witch. It was a man. His face was pale and his expression was blank. His eyes stared straight ahead. He looked familiar.

"Martin Page!" I said, shocked. "You're alive!"

"He is not alive, and he is not dead," said Myles. "He is in between. He cannot talk. He cannot think on his own. He must obey orders. He must do my bidding."

"Oh, my Lord," I muttered, gazing in horror at the undead body of Father Page. I remembered that King James wrote about this in his book, *Demonology*. He described a type of undead human he called "the most curious sort." I assumed it was just a Scottish superstition. But there he stood before me.

"That's impossible," I said, struggling to understand.

"Your own Bible speaks of it," said Myles. "*And the graves were opened, and many bodies of the saints which slept arose, and came out of their graves after the resurrection, and went into the holy city and appeared to many.*"

"That's not what it means," I protested. "It can't be."

"Who are you to lecture me about matters of the spirit?" asked Myles. "The witch cult is the ancient religion of this land. We have been here for centuries, worshiping the horned god and the triple goddess. Dancing at night before the full moon. Until your kind came."

"What you have done is unnatural," I said. "You have trapped his spirit here in the mortal plane. His soul longs for heaven."

"Enough talk," said Myles. "You need not worry. We will not keep your soul here on earth for a moment longer."

"Wait!" I said.

"Martin, bring me the boline," said Myles.

The undead body of Martin Page lumbered out of my view. He returned a moment later with a white-handled knife. It had a curved blade shaped like a crescent moon. He placed it into Myles' waiting hand.

The chanting resumed. The robed witches proceeded walking in a circle around the stone table upon which I was tied.

Astarte, Isis, Diana,
Demeter, Hecate, Kali, Inanna.
Astarte, Isis, Diana,
Demeter, Hecate, Kali, Inanna.

"Help!" I screamed. "Please, someone help me!"

The witches continued circling the table, chanting. My head continued to swim. The walls changed colors and swirled in strange patterns. Sick to my stomach, I felt like I was going to pass out. "Help me!" I screamed in desperation.

Myles stopped on my left side and moved close to the table. The witches stopped and stood silently in the outer circle. He held the knife high in the air and the curved blade shone in the candlelight. He prayed aloud in a language I had never heard, holding the boline above my heart. "William Shakespeare," said Myles in English. "In the name of the great horned god, I send you to the other side!"

His hand tightened as he plunged the knife down towards my waiting chest. A deafening explosion rang out, and the room filled with smoke. Blood dripped from Myles's mouth as he fell upon me, the knife dropping from his hand and clattering on the floor. Myles's lifeless body lay upon me. The witch who was standing behind Myles pulled him off of me. He was holding the wheel-lock pistol I had stashed in my clothes and was standing in a cloud of smoke. He pulled back his hood. The last thing I saw before passing out was my rescuer's face.

It was Edward.

CHAPTER TWENTY-TWO

"The mind is a funny thing," said Doctor Butler, checking my eyes. "It can do strange things when it's under duress. You have no memories of how you got to my examination room?"

"I'm afraid not," I said, shaking my head. I glanced at Judith, her eyes heavy with worry. "Thank you for sending for my daughter."

Doctor Butler nodded. He walked over to a water basin, washed his hands, and dried them on a white towel. He seemed lost in thought. After a moment, he returned to the examination table.

"Well," he said, "from the look of you, it's obvious they drugged you. That may explain some things."

"What do you mean?" asked Judith.

"Certain medicines can make the mind see things that aren't there."

"Like the walls dripping?" I asked.

"Yes," said Doctor Butler.

"Or Martin Page being undead?" asked Judith.

"Perhaps," said the physician. "But there's one thing I can tell you from practicing medicine for so many years. The world is both stranger than we know, and stranger than we can know."

A knock came at the door and Doctor Butler answered. After a moment, Oliver Fletcher and Samantha Winston came into the room.

"Oh, my friends," I said. "I'm so glad you're here."

"Judith sent word to us," said Samantha. "We came as soon as we heard."

"We're so glad you're all right," said Oliver.

"I've been better," I said, and grinned. "But thank you."

"May I give you some good news?" Samantha said, her eyes shining.

"I'd love some good news."

She glanced at Oliver and smiled. "We're going to be married."

"That is exciting news," I said, smiling back at them. "What's next for you two?"

"John Reynolds asked Oliver to help him work on a new English translation of the Bible. With King James' permission, of course. After that, we will go back to Oliver's parish," said Samantha. "We will work together to bring healing to both sides of this religious struggle."

"A wonderful plan," I said. "I wish you the best."

Samantha came to me and gave me a hug.

"Thank you," she said, "for giving me the chance to be an actor. What I learned while acting with the *King's Men* will serve me well no matter what I do in life."

"I'm sure it will," I said, smiling. "Over the past few days, I learned that the skills of an actor have a much broader application than I had realized."

"Thank you," said Oliver, shaking my hand. "I'm afraid we must go, but we wanted to check on you. God bless you, my friend."

"I need to go too," I said. "I have to report to the king and finally put this adventure behind me."

*****

Standing in the Great Watching Chamber, I remembered that this was the room where my adventure really began. As I gazed around the chamber, spacious and beautiful, I smiled. King James sat before the fire in a plush velvet chair.

"Would you like a glass of wine?" asked the king.

"No thank you, Your Majesty," I said. "After last night, I don't suppose I will sample wine for quite some time."

"What do you mean?"

I told King James the whole story. He listened attentively and asked for clarification on a few points. He seemed fascinated that Anne had created the role of Ravynna, and how we used it to gain information.

"Well done, William," said the king at last. "My guards will take over from here. They will make arrests and seal off the rooms you discovered."

The king shook his head. "I never even suspected Myles. He was a great servant. Very loyal. Very attentive. Too attentive, come to think of it. But his thirst for revenge cost him his life. Yes, well done indeed. I must say, this turned out better than I ever imagined."

"Yes, my lord," I said. "But my heart goes out to the priest, Martin Page. Seeing that kind man reduced to a mindless slave broke my heart."

"Yes," said King James, shaking his head. "It would've been better if the poison had killed him. Bringing his body back without his mind was perhaps the cruelest thing the witch cult did. You can rest assured that he will be well cared for. We owe him that. You did excellent work on this assignment, Will."

"I'm glad to be finished with it, Your Majesty," I said. "By your leave, I will return to my room and sleep."

I bowed and walked across the plush carpet to the door. As I turned the doorknob, the king called my name.

"William," the king said. "One more thing."

"Yes, my lord?"

"I have a meeting to attend," he said. "And I would like you to come with me."

King James stood and walked over to a bookcase. He pulled a book out and there was the sound of a mechanism releasing. He pushed against the right side of the bookcase, and it opened. It was a doorway. Stairs led downward and torches blazed on the walls of the stairwell.

"Follow me, please."

We descended the stairs, and my stomach tightened. The air smelled fresh, not stale like the other underground lairs of the palace. At the bottom of the stairs, the room widened. Several passageways led in various directions. The room was well-lit with torches.

"Your Majesty, where are we going?"

"We are almost there," he said. "This way."

We walked down one passageway and came to a heavy wooden door. The king knocked hard three times, followed by two soft knocks, and waited. After a moment, the door opened to a well-lit room. At the center of the room was a large oak table, surrounded by six chairs. Sitting around the table were faces I recognized.

"Please come in, William," said Archbishop Whitgift.

"Thank you, your grace," I said, entering the room.

"Please," said John Reynolds, "have a seat."

King James took his seat at the head of the table. I sat on his right and glanced around the room. The anti-puritan, Richard Bancroft, sat across from me. Next to him was the sexton, Alban Braunstone.

"Alban," I said, surprised to find him among such distinguished company.

"Welcome to King Henry's secret room," said Alban, and smiled.

"Alban is our technical advisor," said the Archbishop.

"Advisor?" I asked.

"Yes," said Whitgift. "Alban has picked up a lot of occult information over the years, some of which is quite useful in this line of work."

"And some of which is clearly heresy," said John Reynolds.

"But useful, nonetheless," said the king.

Three loud knocks followed by two quiet ones sounded on the door.

"Enter," said the king.

The door opened, and in walked Edward Wilkerson.

"Edward," I said, and stood up. "Your Majesty, arrest that man!"

"Relax, William," said the king. "Edward has been a part of our secret society since the beginning."

"Secret society?" I asked.

"Yes," said the king. "Edward has been working undercover for us. He was already investigating witchcraft at the palace when Myles Lewis tried to kill me. You were merely meant to be a distraction, to keep attention focused away from Edward's work."

"I'm sorry I had to pull my gun on you and Anne," said Edward. "But when you confessed that you were only pretending that she was the Witch Queen of England, it was my duty to arrest you both." Edward smiled. "The king frowns on mere mortals usurping his throne."

"But why were you following me through the darkness the day before?" I asked.

"I didn't know it was you," said Edward. "I had lost my light while looking for clues. I heard something moving in the darkness, so I went towards it to investigate."

"You heard something, and you went towards it," I said, feeling a twinge of shame. "I heard something, and I went away from it. You are a braver man than I am, sir."

"But you turned out to be very good at investigating," said Edward, smiling. "You did better than I did."

"Yes," said the king. "So good, in fact, that we want you to continue working for us."

"I don't understand," I said.

"William," said Alban. "There are powers at work in this world beyond your comprehension."

"And there are creatures who prowl the night who would make your blood turn to ice," said Reynolds.

"Will," said King James. "I've handpicked this team to oversee the investigation of many dark forces at work in the British Isles."

"Dark forces?" I asked.

"Yes," said the archbishop. "Witchcraft is only the beginning."

"There are men who turn into wolves when the moon is full," said the king. "And night crawlers who stalk the living."

"And in Scotland," said Reynolds, "there is a water dragon who lives in Loch Ness."

"There are necromancers who can raise the dead," said Bancroft. He looked at the king. "They could turn them into an undead army to take England by force."

"Or so they say," said Alban.

"Yes," said Whitgift. "Or so they say."

"That's where we come in," said Edward.

"William," said the king. "You will be our chief investigator of these matters. You will explore these mysteries and many others, and report back."

Stunned, I sat in silence for a moment.

"William," said the king. "Do you accept your new assignment?"

"I can't, Your Majesty," I said, my mind spinning from all this information. "I have work to do. I have a family to support. I have to earn a living. And we have the play to perform tonight—"

"Never mind that," said the king. "Richard Burbage can handle that. And your new job will pay well. You might even become a rich man."

"If you live long enough," said Edward.

"You will return to London under the pretense of writing one of your plays," said the king, ignoring Edward's remark. "Which you will write as a cover to keep your real work a secret. But you will actually be working for me."

"But—" I said, but the king cut me off.

"Will," said King James, and he stared at me with his penetrating eyes. "I was only asking to be polite. I am your king. This is your new assignment. Do I make myself clear?"

"Yes, Your Highness," I said. "But what about the plague?"

"I'm sure you'll be fine," said the king. "Leave tonight for London."

"What's my first assignment?" I asked.

"There is a group of vampires there who are being murdered," said the king. "Investigate the murders. Find out who is doing it and why."

"And stop them," said the archbishop, "by any means necessary."

"The *vampires* are being murdered?" I asked, struggling to understand.

"Alleged vampires," said Edward.

"Why does His Majesty care if vampires are being murdered?"

"William," said Alban. "Things are not always what they seem."

***

Richard Burbage helped me load the carriage for my trip. We tied the luggage down, and I told him about my new assignment for the king.

"And you have to leave tonight?" he asked, tightening a knot.

"I'm afraid so," I said. "I tried to talk Anne and Judith into staying here, but they both insisted on coming with me to support me in my work. In fact, Judith seems to love the idea of solving another mystery."

Anne, Judith, and Susanna entered the courtyard. Anne and Judith wore their grey woolen travelling coats and matching bonnets. Dressed in a light-brown frock coat, Susanna linked arms with her sister. Her flaxen hair flowed in the icy winter air.

"By the way," I said to Richard, scratching my beard. "I have an idea for a new play. It's about a Scottish general named Macbeth. Three witches prophesy that he will become king one day. But trouble ensues when his wife encourages him to take matters into his own hands."

"I want to play Macbeth!" said Richard, a big smile spreading across his bearded face. "He's the lead, right?"

Laughing, I hugged my old friend goodbye. Anne and the girls walked up to us.

"I'm going to miss you!" said Anne, hugging Susanna tight.

"I'll miss you to," said Susanna. "I'm glad we had a little time together."

"You're staying here?" I asked Susanna.

"Yes," she said, grinning. "The palace needs a new herbalist. I've convinced them that I am an expert in medicinal matters. Now, I need to research my new role."

"Doctor Butler and Alban Braunstone can help you do that," I said, smiling at both my children.

"You're going to miss all the fun," said Judith, hugging her sister. "We're going to have another grand adventure!"

We climbed into the wagon and waved goodbye, ready to leave for London. The coachmen cracked the reins on the backs of the horses, and we were off. We bounced along, and I looked back at Hampton Court Palace. I thought of all of our adventures there, and all the ones to come. I noticed someone watching us from a palace window. Recognizing her, I waved, and she waved back.

"Who's that, dear?" asked Anne.

"Her name is Sybil Penn," I said, and settled back into my seat.

Horse hooves clicked against the cobblestone street. Hickory smoke laced the afternoon air. As I ran my fingers through my hair, I noticed Anne looking at me for more information. I shrugged my shoulders.

"She's a ghost."

THE END

ABOUT THE AUTHOR

Greg Hoover, an award-winning writer, has been an actor, playwright, therapist, and priest. He and his wife have four children, and live surrounded by nature in their country home. Greg loves the outdoors, hiking, exploring, traveling, and playing guitar. *The Witching of the King* is his debut novel.

Note From The Author

Word-of-mouth is crucial for any author to succeed. If you enjoyed *The Witching of the King*, please leave a review online—anywhere you are able. Even if it's just a sentence or two. It would make all the difference and would be very much appreciated.

Thanks!
Greg Hoover

Thank you so much for reading one of our

Occult / Supernatural novels.

If you enjoyed the experience, please check out our
recommendation for your next great read!

Absolute Darkness by Tina O'Hailey

"Tina O'Hailey nails it. She has a great talent, a gift. Character
development is exceptional, the scenes are set so carefully that I
found myself immersed in each."

–Ken Bangs, author of *Guardians in Blue*

View other Black Rose Writing titles at
www.blackrosewriting.com/books and use promo code
PRINT to receive a **20% discount** when purchasing.